Emotionally Bulletproof - Scott's Story

By Brian Shaul and David Allen

Acknowledgements

We want to thank certain individuals who have embraced the Emotionally Bulletproof principles.

Thank you to Joel and Ashlee Starn, for the word-smithing they did for this book series.

Eric and Angela Carlson for the months of helping refine these ideas.

Thank you John and Marlys Hall, for their assistance in editing the original manuscripts and openly sharing these ideas with so many people.

Thank you Janette Riehle for your advice and editing expertise.

Thank you Tim Carrick for being Pastor Tim.

Seek First to Understand

My name is Scott. The authors are about to reveal intricate details of my life, and I insisted on having the chance to speak my part before you read it. I wanted to give you a few words to keep in mind before you read.

I am going to speak to you like you are one of my closest friends. Since you will hear all about what happened to me, I trust you, and don't mind if you tell all your friends about my story. In fact, I hope you do.

First, a little background:

I was born in Wasilla, Alaska and went to public school. My dad's name is Robert, and he is a psychologist. He loves to diagnose. Being in a position of dispensing wisdom was more important to him than actually having wisdom to begin with. Anyway, I grew up with him, my older brother, Phillip, and my mom in a fairly large house outside of town.

My uncle, Matthew, was my favorite person in the world to hang out with. He taught me things you will read about in this book. When he died, I was very angry with God for taking away my favorite person in the world and became a bit of a troublemaker as a teenager. After several years of issues arising from rebellion, it took the help of a pastor named Tim to help me straighten up and begin the part of my journey that I want you to know about.

My brother seemed to have no problem following in the footsteps of my dad and going to college for psychology as well. I, however, noticed that for all the bragging about how successful my family was, they weren't always very happy. Looking back, that's what it was, but at that age I couldn't quite explain it. For this reason, I chose a different path in life, one that was unconventional for them. It caused a lot of tension between me and the rest of my family.

Enough of that. I have no regrets about that part of my past. It was all for the glory of God so that you could hear this story today. Now that you know a bit about me, there are several things I hope you take away from my story.

First: Enjoy the book. Stories are meant to be enjoyed.

Second: Even though I am a fictional character, I hope I can connect parts of what you read with how you experience real life. I know I'm not supposed to just come out and say that, but it's too important not to say.

My story happened years ago, and I know that you have different challenges facing you than what I faced at your age. Families are even more broken. Financial challenges that people never faced when I was your age are in front of you. In times of such uncertainty, we cannot cling only to things. We must instead focus on principles; lifelong truths that have served all who focus on them since the beginning of time.

This story is about my journey to discovering one of these truths. As you read my story, you will learn about trust, the foundation of all relationships. Without it, you won't know how well you are helping others, nor will you know how others can help you, or even if they want to. Pay close attention to trust as you read about my life.

By focusing on the actions of each character and determining whether those actions lay within the three key aspects of trust, you will be able to apply this principle of truth to your own life.

Many of you who read this may have trouble with relationships, whether the trouble is with getting a relationship in the first place, or keeping it after you get it.

Others still have trouble with money. Maybe you need to make more to achieve your dreams than you are currently capable of making. Maybe you're drowning in debt.

Lastly, you may just need support in times of instability. Believe me, I've been there.

All aspects of your life require a high amount of trust, both with yourself and those you associate with. All those areas will improve with successful practicing of trust. Try to see if anyone in my story seems similar to people in your own. If not, use what you learn about trust to make your own decisions.

If you want to use this book as a self-help book, you will probably want to finish this chapter. If you are reading it only for entertainment purposes, I'm going to get a bit preachy in the rest of this chapter, so go ahead and begin the story in Chapter 1.

In developing your trust and taking it to a higher level, you must be aware of certain mindsets that may cause problems when you try to make change. By being aware, we can act in spite of those paradigms and make a true improvement. I have taken some of the common issues I have seen and described them here for you.

Blaming - When people learn about trust, they begin to see examples in the world around them of trust and mistrust in action. You will see it in your church, your family, your friends, your school, your government, and your town. Your awareness is going to sharply increase, as you will see the direct result of low trust and high trust environments and their consequences. This is normal and healthy. It is part of the learning process for you.

Before you run to your pastor and confront him, before you scream at your wife, and before you point the finger at your employees, stop and think: How will people unaware of trust issues respond to accusation? Will they say, "Oh, I've never thought about it that way. Please tell me how to change!"? Will they bow in humility when you proclaim your newfound truth? While you may have visualized that type of reaction, the reality is that blaming someone else will be seen as denying your own responsibility for the situation. They will likely respond by confronting you with the same intensity and emotions that you sent their way.

There are ways to bring about their awareness without acting like a prosecuting attorney or talking like a victim. I challenge you, before trying to influence others, to take a look at yourself. A high trust or low trust environment is just that, an environment. You are part of the environment too.

In the Bible, a passage is written that has the same relevance today as it did when it was written, and accurately gives counsel on this issue. "How can you think of saying, 'Friend, let me help you get rid of that speck in your eye,' when you can't see past the log in your own eye? Hypocrite! First get rid of the log in your own eye; then you will see well enough to deal with the speck in your friend's eye." I believe it was Luke 6:42, or somewhere around there.

In short, always look towards improving your own level of trust first.

Deception - When someone has lied to you and you believe it, you start acting on that lie as if it were true. Telling someone about this is challenging, because doing so will usually get the response of "I'm not deceived." Let me ask you something. If you know someone is lying to you, can they deceive you? No. You have to believe a lie to be deceived. You won't believe a liar knowingly, at least I hope you don't. You can only be deceived by not being aware of the deception.

Remember the previous section on blaming, and be aware that we all have been deceived. Deception happens to everyone. The best way to combat deception is to form a group of people who all seek to improve their trust, and discuss it with them. Some of these people will have an area of strength that you may be lacking, and they will be able to see things that you could not on your own. This guidance is priceless. Be careful whose advice you accept, though, and be careful which advice you apply.

1 John 4:1 says, "Dear friends, do not believe everyone who claims to speak by the Spirit. You must test them to see if the spirit they have comes from God. For there are many false prophets in the world."

Many people who speak falsely may do so out of the best intentions, yet may also be deceived themselves. In all situations, look for the truth, and don't be afraid of being wrong.

Pride - This one ties into deception and blaming as well. I want to discuss pride for two reasons: to lower pride so that you may face the truth and get out of deceiving yourself, and so that you may keep the influence and trust you have won.

Let's go over lowering pride. When increasing trust, try your best not to attack those who challenge you with an idea. Doing so is a way of communicating pride. If you're fortunate, the person challenging you is trustworthy enough to know when you are feeling defensive. More than likely, though, the people who can help you grow will become discouraged and stop trying to help you on your journey. If you burn bridges and scare away people who want to free you from deception, you are isolating yourself with those who are deceiving you. In short, pride causes you to deceive yourself. So stop it.

With all the deception in the world, the 'Main Deceiver' doesn't need your help.

Now for the next reason. Listen when I say this: I am NOT an expert! If I refer to myself as the expert on trust, there is a danger that I might stop trying to grow personally. If that happens, think of my family, friends, employees, and students who look up to me. If they see me as the expert on trust, and I do nothing to improve myself, they will imitate me so that they, too, will become experts. This will cause my family to suffer, my employees to lose motivation, and my church to stop growing. Do you really want to think of yourself as the expert? Do you want to be responsible for all those negative consequences affecting so many people? I wouldn't go to a church full of 'experts' if I could avoid it.

Lack of Healthy Boundaries - It is here that you need to know one of the legs of trust. *Having other people's best interests in mind.* I bring it up because you may find someone who wants to hog your mind, to be the only source of advice and council for you. They may seem to have it all together, and people talk in public about how great they are. It may be because they have high trust in several areas.

It is important that you develop multiple sources of advice. Study truth with more than just one person. If that one person or group seeks to keep you from learning anywhere else, there may be a conflict of interest. Their desire to control may be higher than their desire for you to grow as a person. Every aspect of trust ties together, so if this is the case, you will often find a lack of trust in another area of their life. Read the story and you will discover what those legs of trust are.

I want to leave it up to you to find out more. This principle of trust can be applied anywhere to achieve results, and its options are without limit. When you do find how to use it, tell me one day. I need this information more than ever!

Before I let the authors take over, I wanted to leave a gift with you, which you'll find at the end of the book. You see, I learned from mistakes made by me and those around me. The authors put me through much agony to learn this. It made me wish I had a guide to help me understand trust; something that I can share with others, so we all could have each other's best interests in mind. Well, the authors worked with me to make one, and I am proud to present it to you. After you read, you can fill out the papers or make copies so that you can use what I learned to improve the quality of your own life.

Now I turn it over to the authors, finishing by saying three words I wish upon everyone: God Bless You!

Discussion Questions
For Each Chapter

On this page you will find five questions you can use when studying my story with others. You can use those questions to learn more about trust, and discuss it with others so they can grow too. If you don't know the three aspects of trust yet, you can look at the back of the book where the worksheets are. I know, I said you have to read to find out, but I care more about you learning than whether or not you read about me. Cheating is encouraged in this special case.

How was Scott affected in a negative way by trusting somebody who scored low on trust?

Did Scott have the three legs of trust for himself in this chapter?

How was Scott affected in a positive way by trusting somebody who scored high on trust?

Can you remember a time in the last week when you were blessed by somebody having the three aspects of trust?

In the next week, which of the three aspects of trust are you going to focus on improving?

Chapter 1

The door slammed, echoing behind Scott. He trotted through the dimly lit gym. Outside, large palm fronds hung across the windows, blocking the light, creating a speckled pattern across the concrete floor.

"Tony," Scott hissed. "Tony."

"What?" Tony turned, tossing his blond hair. "What's the problem?" He leaned on his mop, annoyance in his voice. "I'm trying to work here." He stood, legs apart, wearing a pair of cutoff shorts, eyeing Scott suspiciously.

Scott stopped, panting to catch his breath. "You really need to get out of here Tony." He gulped air. "Tai, he's drunk and very angry. He's coming with some friends to beat you up." He glanced behind him. "He has a machete."

"Ha!" Tony looked uncertain. "Probably because you gave him one." He spun toward Scott, eyes narrowing. "What'd you tell Tai? I know you're still trying to get back at me for Janet." He gripped his mop and stepped forward. "Don't pretend that you're innocent."

"Tony, stop being stupid. I told them nothing. Abra told me to run and tell you quickly." Scott motioned desperately. "Hurry! Go, you're alone in this gym and they're coming on the road behind me. I cut across the island to get ahead of them."

"How do I know you're not sending me into a trap?" Tony's face was a mask of distrust. "I'll do no such thing. I'm not afraid of a couple of stumbling drunks." He began to turn away.

Scott made one final effort, reaching out and grabbing his sleeve. "Tony there's five of —" *Boom!* The gym's front door was flung open. Five sullen islanders stepped through the door, three of them clutching short wooden clubs.

Tony shook Scott off with an angry twist, and then stepped back uncertainly. Tai stood in the middle, long, unkempt black hair framing his dark countenance. He glared at Tony through bloodshot eyes. A machete hung from his stocky waist.

"You pig." He spat. The doors swung closed behind the islanders with a slow metallic click. "You insulted my little sister." Tai walked slowly across the hard floor. His cloth sandals slapped the ground as he walked. He clenched and unclenched his fist slowly. The semi-circle of men advanced behind him, eliminating Tony's chance of escape. "And you killed Janet," Tai accused.

"I did no such thing!" Tony roared. He balanced on his tiptoes, facing Tai. He waved his muscular arm. "The woman drowned because she couldn't swim."

Tai wasn't fazed. "You let her drown, because you are a selfish pig." He paused for effect. "That's right, a selfish pig," he repeated slowly.

"Look, you idiot!" Tony yelled, lifting his mop handle threateningly. " I'll knock your lights out if you don't get out of my face!" His neck showed red around the collar. He clearly was not trying to be diplomatic.

A soft chuckle rose from one of the men.

"What did you say?" Tai cocked his head questioningly. He took another step. "You really think you can knock all our lights out?"

Tony swayed as he glanced rapidly from face to face. "Ya, ya I will," he sputtered, face red.

A row of wooden chairs stood to the side behind Tony. Scott saw them as his brain searched frantically for an escape. An idea jumped into his mind. He stepped to the right and grabbed the closest chair by its wooden legs with a swift movement. He quickly raised it above his head and smashed it on the concrete floor with a splintering thud. Pieces of wood skittered across the floor. Everyone stood frozen in place, staring at Scott, mouths agape. Tony turned and stared at Scott incredulously. Scott stood up, holding one of the thick chair legs. Tai stepped back, uncertain, and Tony stepped after him with new confidence.

"That's right, you stupid drunk! Scott here will crack your thick coconut head with his —"

Crack! Scott swung the leg of the chair with a smooth motion. It came flying from the side and hit Tony in the head with a hollow thump. Tony dropped his mop and fell sagging onto the floor, blood oozing from the side of his head. Scott stepped firmly on his back.

"Yeah!" Tai said, seizing the opportunity. He liked the sudden turning of events. He stepped forward clenching his fist.

"Tai, Stop!" Scott barked.

Tai stepped back, confused by the change. "Why?" he challenged.

The group of men stood facing Scott, dumbfounded. Hadn't he just knocked Tony down?

"I've already knocked him out! Do you want to be responsible for murdering an American?"

Tai shook his head and glared back. "We won't kill him, just rough him up a bit," Tai said. "He insulted my sister!"

Tony raised his head from the floor. "You're stupid —" he began to sputter.

Scott pushed the heel of his foot into Tony's head, pushing his face into the dirty mop.

"Be quiet!" Scott commanded.

"See? I should cut his tongue out!" Tai yelled.

Scott realized that he was the only thing standing between Tony and this angry man. "No, you shouldn't." He looked calmly at Tai and spoke evenly. "If you touch him, you'll go to prison, and if anything happens to him, I'm certain this mission school will be shut down." He looked from Tai to the island men. "Do you want to be responsible for the loss of your island's education?" Scott ground Tony's face deeper into the mop. Tony didn't resist this time.

"You're right, Teacher," Tai said grudgingly. "We don't want the mission to close down."

The rest of the men shook their heads. "No, Teacher, we have children in school. We don't want that."

Tai let go of his machete. "I guess you already have sat down the chair on his arrogant mouth." He turned to his cohorts, and they grunted their approval. "I hope that dirty mop reminds his mouth to never insult my sister again."

Scott kept his foot pressed on Tony's head. "You all go, before someone gets in trouble." He spoke in a controlled tone, realizing that his reason was the only way he could protect Tony. The adrenaline was still pumping.

"Okay, Teacher, but only because you did the right thing by hitting him." Tai didn't want to lose face, but he was already backing toward the gym door. A chorus of approval rose from the men. "You did right, Teacher." With that, the men turned and walked out of the gym laughing.

Scott kept his foot on Tony's head until they all left. As the gym door clicked shut, he lifted his foot off Tony and reached out his hand, "Are you okay, Tony? Let me help you up."

Tony rolled away angrily. "I'll be fine." He shoved Scott's hand away. "Leave me alone! I don't want your help." He staggered to his feet, wiping blood and dirt from his face. He ran, stumbling, out the gym's back door.

Scott didn't follow. He slumped to the floor, feeling exhausted as the realization of what he'd just done sank in. In a strange twist, he had just saved Tony's life.

*****

Scott sat on the beach, watching the distant waves break over the reef. He appeared to be deep in thought, and did not notice the man jogging toward him through the coconut palms.

"Scott!" the man panted. "I finally found you." Scott turned, startled, looking up into the runner's sweating face. "I've looked all over this island for you." He plopped down on the sand, his chest heaving.

"Jerry. I thought no one could find me here." Scott appeared irritated for a second, but then he couldn't hide that he was glad to see his friend.

Jerry looked at him with concern. "You've needed a lot of time since the *Santa Maria* sank." There was silence between the two friends for a second, then Jerry continued. "Abra agreed to take me out shark fishing tonight. I'd really like to have you go with me. I've never failed to catch sharks with you; you have a knack. Plus, it would probably be good for you to get off this island after what just happened."

Scott spoke as if he hadn't heard the invitation. "I'm sorry I've been this way, I just took the accident very hard. I don't want to be around Tony, either."

Jerry was quiet for a second. "We all took it hard, Scott."

Anyone looking in over the sparkling reef could see the pair sitting in the white sand. Scott with his red afro and troubled blue eyes, sitting next to some cracked coconut shells, his freckled skin a victim of the intense Marshall Island sun. He was 20 and in his prime. He hadn't completely filled out yet, but he looked tough. Jerry was tall with long brown hair, which was stuck to his forehead. He wiped it away with a movement of his arm.

"We'll need to get some blood and guts, then," Scott said. "The tide will be going out soon, and we need to draw the sharks in. We should go to the bottleneck in Bigei lagoon." He jumped up. His thoughts were now focused, energized.

Jerry followed him through the palms. "Wait up, Scott! I just ran all the way out here. You've been resting on the beach!"

*****

The bucket of guts from the cannery sloshed as Scott waved away the flies. "Perfect. Nice and strong. If flies like the smell, the sharks will too." He handed the second bucket to Jerry. "Let's go find Abra."

The pair made their way down the coral sand street, past concrete brick homes with thatched roofs. Chickens pecked in the street underneath the palm trees.

"Let's go this way," Scott turned down a path toward the beach.

Jerry raised an eyebrow. "That way's longer, you're just trying to avoid Tony," he observed.

"And so what if I am trying to avoid him?" Scott gripped his pole. "I want to concentrate on fishing."

The two arrived at the dock, just in time to meet Abra.

"It's very kind of you to take us out." Scott reached out and shook the older native man's hand.

Abra had spear fished these waters for many years and possessed a priceless knowledge of the reef.

"I'll take you to the head of Bigei lagoon, where all the deep water flows when the tide returns. I see you have your chum, so is there anything else you need before we go?" Abra asked.

"We have everything we need here." Jerry pointed to a stack of snorkels, and duffle bags.

"Okay, Van Damme, let's get you off this island before any more chairs get broke." Abra gave Scott a meaningful wink.

Scott coughed and Jerry punched him in the shoulder playfully. Scott swung his fins into the boat. "I just don't want to be hanging around him if he starts thinking about it too much." The three men chuckled. It was the start of a good fishing trip.

The ride to the next island lasted about 45 minutes. Scott sat in the front of the boat and pointed out dolphins racing like streamlined torpedoes through the crystal water. This was the dolphins' hunting grounds, and today the playful dolphins took a break to chase the speeding boat. The dolphins turned away as the boat approached the beach.

They pulled up along the side of a concrete pier left behind from the second World War. Scott and Jerry unloaded the camping equipment onto the beach while Abra followed close behind with the buckets of fish guts.

"Okay, this is it. I'll see you boys tomorrow evening about this time. Things should be calmed down with Tony by then." Abra waved as Scott and Jerry pushed the boat free of the pier. "Happy fishing," Abra yelled.

Scott found a place on the beach high enough that the big waves wouldn't reach their gear. He lugged his duffel bag to the chosen spot. Jerry gathered coconut husks for a fire that night.

"The tide won't be going out for another 90 minutes or so," Jerry said, dumping an armload of fibrous husks. "Why don't we go out snorkeling first? I have something I want to show you. It's just before the drop off, you'll be amazed."

Scott looked up at Jerry, curious. The guy was always full of surprises. "Sounds good to me. I'll take my spear gun along, too. Maybe we'll see some jack tuna for dinner tonight." Scott reached into the duffel bag and pulled out his gun and fins.

The two friends waded out through the foaming surf together. Scott sloshed ahead and dove into a small green wave with a whoop, and then rolled over to adjust his mask and snorkel. Scott then sunk into the water and kicked out toward the dropoff.

The depth increased to about ten feet as they paddled out. Small aquatic grasses grew between the large coral heads as they neared the deeper water. A skate scurried to the cover of the reef as the two men swam over. Large schools of jack tuna, grouper and angelfish swam lazily through the water, looking with mild curiosity at the two strange creatures paddling through their world. Jerry waved Scott out into deeper water and pointed to a strange structure in the smooth sand. Scott peered into the blue. What was that? Surely not a reef. He swam forward and then saw a line of metal ribs. It wasn't coral... no, it was a plane. The outline of an old aircraft lay on the bottom. Small fish swam through its struts, and fan coral waved smoothly from its fuselage. It had been there a while. Jerry tapped him on the shoulder, pulling him to the surface.

"It's an old Japanese Zero. I found it last year, snorkeling with Abra, Probably sat there at least 50 years." Jerry treaded water.

Scott looked down at the strange plane below. A couple of ragged holes showed on one collapsed wing. He rolled over, and dove down to take a better look, his muscular legs propelling him deeper into the blue. He could feel the pressure increasing as he descended; he let a stream of bubbles race to the sun above. A black fish darted from the cockpit as he neared. Scott peered in. Only the metal remained, covered with sand and algae. It was dim. Smashed, unidentifiable instruments were mixed with rust and gunk.

I wonder if the pilot died? The thought wandered through Scott's mind dreamily. Had the pilot been captured, or had he bailed out over the water? Did the aviator drift at sea? Did the navy search for him? Did...did he have a sweetheart? Scott instinctively closed his eyes at the thought. He could see tangled brunette hair holding Janet's lifeless body under the surface ... Scott opened his eyes, there was nothing there except for the silent plane in front of him. It was just a flashback. He jerked away, kicking up toward the sparkling surface, out of the depths. He felt the pressure releasing. His head shot up and he gasped for air.

"You look green. Did you swallow sea water?" Jerry looked at him amused.

Scott breathed hard. "Am I pale? It just...it just reminded me of Janet, that's all."

"Everything reminds you of Janet!"

Scott flipped his mask off with a twist of his wrist, and rolled onto his back, resting. "Let's go to shore, I don't want to snorkel anymore," he muttered.

"Okay." Jerry shrugged, turning in the water.

*****

The concrete pier Scott sat on was from the same time period as the Zero on the reef. It was solid and had been built on that location because it was the only deep place to anchor in the lagoon. When the war had ended, the pier had been abandoned. The natives had discovered that it was an excellent place to catch sharks and large fish as it was deep, and large volumes of tidal water would pass through the gap in the coral. Put a little chum in the outgoing tide and wait. You would often see the dark shadows of sharks swimming in to investigate.

Scott was baiting his hook with a bloody piece of flesh when Jerry trotted onto the pier with four coconuts. He glanced up. "Why'd you get sprouted coconuts?" He twisted the meat on his hook.

"Watch and learn my friend." Jerry smiled. "When was the last time you had an apple?" He peeled the husk from a coconut.

"It's been a while. Probably Christmas." Scott looked up, one eyebrow raised.

Jerry split the coconut open with a quick swipe of his machete. He reached through the split husk and pulled out the white core. "You eat it just like an apple, it's a little crunchy, too." Jerry handed the round core to Scott. Scott set the pole down, and leaned over the dock to rinse his hands.

Scott bit into the sweet core, delicious and white. "It tastes like a pear-apple."

"It's good isn't it?" Jerry tossed the husk into the blue water. He picked up his pole and made a clean cast. The bait splashed as it hit the water. "We should pour more chum in, the tide's going out." Jerry pointed to the rippling water. Scott slopped half a gallon of the grizzle into the current. "How did the fight happen?" Jerry stood next to Scott. "All I heard was rumors and what Abra told me." He turned expectantly. "I heard there was an uproar at the mission and that you knocked Tony out."

Scott looked away. "I can see why people could say that."

Jerry cleared his throat. "Scott, was it because of Janet?"

Scott flinched. "No it wasn't... well, yes it was." He turned toward Jerry. "You know, I loved Janet." The wind was the only sound for a second, then he continued. "She was the only girl I ever trusted, and... now she's..." His voice broke. "Gone."

Scott's chest moved with silent sobs. He leaned forward, unable to hide his pain.

Jerry stood quietly. Sometimes silence was the best way to understand. Scott sat hunched over, only his red hair moving with the breeze. Jerry was pensive.

"Did you, I mean, is that why you hit Tony?"

"No."

"Are you sure?"

Scott sat up and looked Jerry in the eye. "Yes, I'm sure." Anger flashed in his eyes. "Do you think I would fight out of vengeance? That would only make it worse, and Janet wouldn't have wanted that."

"No, No… it just looks that way." Jerry spread his hands. "What would you say? You hit Tony with the leg of a chair!"

"I know." His voice was shaky. "But that's not the reason. I saved Tony's life, Jerry. That's why I hit him, to save him from Tai."

Jerry shook his head. "I don't understand. What about Janet?"

Scott turned away. "Sometimes only time can heal things. I can't talk about it right now." He leaned on a concrete pillar to steady himself. "I'm sorry about my outburst." He rubbed his face and turned. "The sharks should be coming soon."

*****

The sun was beginning to set, a huge, glowing red ball in the west, its red and orange reflection inky across the lagoon. A pelican flew over the pier. The darkening water lapped at the concrete supports. Sundown in the Pacific fell quickly.

"Good thing we have our mosquito nets." Jerry swatted an early arriver. "The buggers will soon be here in full force."

"I wonder what the Japanese thought when they saw the sun like that." Scott pointed at the setting sun.

"You still thinking about that Zero on the reef?"

"Yes." He squinted at the sun. "I just can't imagine what it would be like to be shot down."

"He could have run out of gas," Jerry suggested.

"I don't understand why people have so many wars."

Jerry turned. "That's kind of a strange thing for you to say, considering what you just did to Tony." He wished he hadn't said it as soon as he saw Scott's expression.

Scott shook his head and turned away. "You don't understand."

The darkness came quickly, but soon a bright moon rose. Scott saw the tide returning. Now they stood with flashlights, scanning the water for sharks. The scent of blood had drifted far in the ocean.

"Hey, look right there!" The two flashlights converged on a slim shadow. "I think that's a shark," Jerry said excitedly, "See he's checking out my bait — I think he's coming back." The shark's silhouette reappeared, making a darting run at the bait.

"Wow! Got 'em!" The pole jerked, *whizzzzz!* The spinner rotated as the shark dove for the bottom. "Come on, play him! Bring him in!" Scott yelled. "Don't let him get wrapped around the pier!"

The shark's tail flailed the water. He moved to the side.

"That's it, tire him out." Scott held his pole in one hand and shone his light where Jerry's line jogged crazy patterns in the water.

"Get him over on that side, okay now."

Wham! Scott's pole was nearly wrenched from his hand. A school of sharks must have come in. Scott jerked back for all he was worth.

"This bad boy's huge!" Scott grunted. He didn't know if his thirty-pound test line would hold. The shark rolled. Scott could see grayish stripes in the moonlight. "I think it's a tiger shark!" he yelled. "I can't get him." The pole was almost being yanked out of Scott's hands by the powerful fish.

Scott let the shark take his line. There was no way he could bring it in without tiring it first. Jerry seemed to have his shark under control, but Scott was being jerked around the dock.

"I can't stay on the pier, I'm going on the beach!" Scott jumped as he was half-yanked from the pier. He landed on the sand, both feet planted in a brace. "Help me, Jerry!" Scott yelled, "You're gonna have to club this guy when I bring him in."

The surf was black and the shark made yet another run to shake the line. Scott felt the powerful pulling and felt his sandals twisting on his feet. He didn't want to trip, so he kicked them off with quick jerks of his feet. He took a couple of steps to balance. Suddenly a sharp pain shot up his leg.

"Umph," Scott gasped, staggering onto his other leg. He was hobbling while still trying to hold onto his rod. He felt the sting of salt water and rough sand in his foot. He must have stepped on something sharp. He winced. It was still in his foot. *Zing!* The line fell slack and Scott could hear a distant splash. The shark had broken his line.

Scott limped out of the wet sand. He walked on his toes because he couldn't put the back of his right foot down. He pulled himself up on the pier and lifted his foot.

"I got him, he's a nice four-foot white tip" Jerry yelled, running up to Scott in the dark. "Hey, what are you doing? Did your shark get away?"

"Yes." Scott grimaced and gripped his foot. "And I stepped on something in the surf, my foot hurts."

Jerry whipped out his flashlight and shone it on Scott's heel. A piece of glass stuck out of an ugly cut on his heel. Red blood dripped from his foot and sand stuck to the wound.

"That's bad. You need to take care of that!" Jerry looked worried.

"Oh, it's nothing. Just looks bad," Scott grimaced as he jerked the glass free. He quickly stuck his thumb on the gash to slow the bleeding.

"There's sand and junk in that, man, we need to clean it." Jerry reached for Scott's foot.

Scott winced. "Let's just rinse it and put a rag on it, don't scrape it!" He jerked his foot away.

"There's sand in there," Jerry protested.

"Look, it's not that bad." Scott pulled himself to a standing position and limped down the pier. "I can walk on it now since it doesn't have glass in it."

"Let's call it a night." Jerry slapped a mosquito. "You can't fish anymore and the bugs are getting worse. I'll release my shark and let's call it a night."

*****

The next morning, Scott looked up at the yellow dome of the tent. He could feel the rising sun's heat through the polyester. A few bugs buzzed and hummed noisily around the outside of the tent. He turned toward a snoring sound. Jerry lay half naked on his side of the tent, mouth open. Scott glanced at his watch—6:43a.m. The sun rose early.

He yawned and unzipped the tent as quietly as he could; no use waking Jerry. Scott stepped one foot out and felt an immediate angry throb. He saw that his foot was red around the wound.

"Ouch!" He hopped on his left foot into the sand. Maybe he should have taken better care of it. Scott unscrewed his water bottle and poured some on the wound. He wrapped his heel in the duct tape he found in the almost empty first aid kit and then slipped his sandal on.

A few minutes later, Jerry crawled out of the tent to find Scott poking a coconut husk fire and eating a banana. "I'll take the breakfast omelet with all the fixings, please, and a glass of orange juice." He stretched.

"Would you like that with ramen or bananas?" Scott asked. He flipped Jerry a ripe banana. "Help yourself, it's an all-you-can-eat buffet."

Jerry sat on a small log and chewed his banana content-edly. "Why don't we hike across the island and look for shells on the ocean side? Abra won't be back until this afternoon."

" I can't." Scott held up his foot. "The duct tape won't hold it together." He grimaced at his attempt at humor.

"What happened?" Jerry asked. "Oh, that's your foot you cut. I told you, you should have taken better care of it."

Scott shook his head. "No, it will be fine. There's a great deal to be said for the body's ability to heal itself, and my foot is no exception." He said with conviction.

"Have you ever heard of matter over mind? Well, some-times nature gets over your mind's idea, especially without help," Jerry quipped.

Scott ignored Jerry's twist of words and watched him rummage in the duffel bag.

"Where's the first aid kit?" Jerry dropped the bag, impatient.

"Right here." Scott pointed to the roll of duct tape. "It's all we have to fix my malady."

Jerry shook his head in disbelief. "Good thing Abra's coming today."

"Let's just pack up camp, maybe Abra will be here by then."

*****

Two days later…

The iridescent clock hands glowed in the darkness: 3:04 a.m. Scott groaned and shook his aching head. What had awakened him? What a horrible dream. Some man, maybe Tony—the face wavered in his tired mind—had punched him just below the waist. It was almost like he really had. Scott reached a hand down and touched it. A painful lump protruded. It throbbed when he put pressure on it, and he drew his hand away.

"Maybe I should just go back to sleep." Scott lay exhausted and sweating in the darkness. He didn't want to wake up the other guys in the apartment.

He touched it again. "Oh." It really hurt. Scott felt a large, sore bulge. He rolled over. "Jerry," he hissed. "Jerry." He leaned across his cot and tapped his sleeping friend on the shoulder.

"What is it?" Jerry pulled the pillow over his head, then sat up and looked at the clock. "It's 3:07, what's the matter?"

"I hurt real bad, I think I have a hernia from fighting that shark." Scott sat on the edge of his bed. "I think you should look at this." Jerry pulled a string connected to the light. A bare bulb shone from the ceiling.

Scott sat on the bed, head down, sweating. He only wore his boxers. His eyes were reddish and he had a pained expression on his face. Jerry squinted at Scott.

"You don't get a hernia two days later. You look weak, here, let me see."

"I want you to feel this." Scott stood and put Jerry's hand slightly below his waist. "Careful!" He winced. Jerry moved his fingers across it.

He looked concerned. "We need to go wake up Director Henrich so his wife can see you."

"That's bad," Scott mumbled sleepily. "The Henrichs don't like being woke up. Is she the only nurse we can reach?"

Jerry nodded from his cot. "Yes, I think so, there's no one else."

Scott pulled on a pair of pants and a shirt and rummaged for his shoes. Jerry helped him up.

"Come on, let's go." The two stumbled out into the dark night, Scott leaning on Jerry.

The walk up the steps of the Henrichs' apartment was difficult for Scott. Jerry helped him up one step at a time.

Jerry knocked loudly on the door. It seemed a full three minutes before the light above the entry switched on. A man in a bathrobe stepped out.

"This had better be good." Director Henrich growled. "It's an ungodly early time to be up."

"Sir." Jerry shifted Scott's arm. "You'd better take a look at Scott, I think he's real sick."

Henrich leaned forward. "What's your ailment, young man?"

"I think, uh, I think I have a hernia, here." Scott pointed. "It hurts real bad."

The director did a quick examination, then put his hand on Scott's forehead.

"You're burning up." He stepped back. "I'll get my wife." Two minutes later the director was back with Elizabeth. "Tell me what you think, Liz." He leaned forward, watching.

"Why are you limping?" Elizabeth touched Scott's wrist with her cool fingers.

"Uh, I cut my foot."

"Let me see." The nurse gently pulled his sandal free. A red line ran from the swollen foot up to his knee, then disappeared. "It's obvious you have an infection. It's traveled up to your lymph glands in your groin." Elizabeth ran an expert finger along the line. "You shouldn't have let this go this long. You need antibiotics bad. When did you get cut?"

"Only a couple days ago, but I figured it wasn't that bad. I only noticed the hernia this morning."

"It's not a hernia, it is an infection," Elizabeth snapped. "We need to get you to a hospital."

Scott nodded numbly. "Jerry, I need to sit down. I feel dizzy."

"Okay." Jerry gripped Scott's arm.

"Bring him inside." Elizabeth quickly stepped ahead, holding the door open.

Scott looked up at her. He felt Mr. Henrich and Jerry lifting him through the door. Everything was fading. He felt so tired...

Chapter 2

"I think he just passed out." Jerry shifted under the weight of Scott's body.

Elizabeth reached out and touched his cheek. "Scott! Scott, can you hear me?" She helped her husband and Jerry lower him onto the couch, then she took over. "Jerry, run and get Abra and another big strong man, and hurry." She turned as Jerry rushed out the door. "Edward, get me a wool blanket."

Ten minutes later Jerry hurried in with Abra and another man. Elizabeth was wiping Scott's forehead with a cloth and Mr. Henrich was talking on the phone.

"Good, good. If you have a bed clear we will be there in just a few minutes. Thank you very much." He hung up. "Okay, the hospital ward has a bed that was just vacated. Let's get him there."

Mr. Henrich opened a drawer and pulled out a pair of keys. "Honey, why don't you stay here and rest?" He paused as he searched for the right key. "The nurse will take good care of him until you get there in the morning."

"Alright." Elizabeth sank to the couch. "Just make sure you tell them to get him antibiotics right away, will you, Edward?" She looked up at her husband.

"Okay, Liz." Mr. Henrich turned to the other three. "Men, I'll get my pickup truck, you three bring him downstairs.

The Rastrojero's rear lights cast a reddish glow over Scott's pale face as they hoisted him into the truck, an island version of an ambulance.

Jerry climbed into the dusty interior and got Scott clear of Henrich's tools. The hatch slammed shut, and he was forced to grip the side for support as Henrich popped the truck into gear. He looked down at Scott. His lips were moving and Jerry heard him mumble something incoherently. He strained to hear, but the sound of the road and the truck rattling drowned out the words.

*****

The Rastrojero ground to a halt outside the small hospital. Abra and the other man climbed from the front seat as Henrich opened the tailgate and looked in. "Jerry, I'll make sure your classes are covered tomorrow. It's been a rough night for you, so I'll take care of everything else."

"Thank you." Jerry's eyes were tired but grateful. "I'll stay here with Scott."

Jerry helped the guys lift Scott from the truck. "He might be waking up. I saw his lips moving on the way here." Jerry lifted Scott's head carefully over the tailgate.

"Probably just delirious," replied Mr. Henrich.

The bare walls of the hospital greeted their tired eyes as they carried Scott through the metal entryway. A smell consisting of bleach mixed with a dim stench filled the stuffy air. A brown cockroach scurried across the floor in front of them as they started down the corridor. Around the corner, they finally met the one overworked hospital aid, who guided them into an empty room. She made a sweeping gesture with her hand.

"I had no time to clean. If you want to clean up first, I don't have a problem with it." Her thick accent did not hide the strain in her voice. She hurried out the door.

Jerry sniffed and lifted his nose away. "Hold on, don't put him on that bed." He looked down at the stained mattress. Obviously the person before must have had loose bowels.

"Flip the mattress over, the man's heavy," Mr. Henrich huffed. The other man shifted to hold more weight. "Better," he panted.

With a heave, Jerry flipped the mattress over, careful to touch the sides only. "This side isn't much better, but at least it doesn't have diarrhea on it."

"It will have to do." Mr. Henrich said. "Put a clean sheet on it."

It was 4:15 AM. The men helped Scott get settled as best they could before they made their exit, leaving him alone with Jerry.

"I'll speak to the nurse on the way out," Mr. Henrich stated. "I'll make sure they get him on a strong antibiotic right away, and if anything gets worse, to call and tell me immediately." Mr. Henrich moved toward the door, then stopped. "My wife will come in the morning. I'll take care of everything at the school for you two." He scratched his balding scalp. "Since Scott's incident with Tony, the school's spirit hasn't been the same — a lot of tension." He looked deep in thought for a second, then stiffened. "We must take utmost care." He looked directly at Jerry. "We cannot have any more incidents. The board is already questioning me about Janet and the accident. Anything more and they will replace me." His gaze moved to Scott. "Take good care of him, we'll all be praying." Mr. Henrich stepped through the door. The sound of his footsteps slowly faded away.

Jerry turned and looked at his delirious friend. "No more incidents?"

Scott looked so helpless and weak right now. Jerry shook his head and turned to gaze into the room. It was bare. A folding chair leaned against one cracked wall. He grabbed it and unfolded it with a squeaking lurch. He sat down, then stood up and walked to the door, restless. He looked up and down the corridor. The same lady bustled back, pushing a cart.

"We'll get him on an IV as soon as the nurse can see him." she called. "I'm sorry, but a woman is in labor right now, and only Kathy is here."

"The doctor isn't here?" Jerry asked, concerned.

"No, he hasn't been to this island for a couple days now. He's due to be back from the outer islands later this morning. I have to go, keep an eye on him and give him some hydration if he wakes." She wiped her hands on her apron, cocking an eyebrow at Jerry. "Is there anything else you need?"

"Where can I get water for Scott?" Jerry looked back in the door, "There isn't a sink or water in there."

"In the washroom."

"Where's the washroom?"

"End of the hall, to your left." She reached into her cart and pulled something free from a bag. "Here's a paper cup."

She turned and rushed the cart away. Jerry sighed, and glanced back at Scott, still the same, limp and sleeping with an occasional twitch. Jerry walked down the hall to the bathroom.

Jerry returned with a cup of lukewarm water and tried unsuccessfully to help Scott drink. Most of the liquid ran down his cheeks and to the pillow. It wasn't easy making an unconscious person drink. Jerry set the cup on the empty counter. He felt tired. He yawned, cupping his head in his hands. His back hurt sitting in the rigid chair. What was taking them so long, anyway?

Shouldn't the nurse have come by now? He leaned the chair backwards so that only two wobbling legs supported him. His eyes closed.

"Don't go." A voice rasped. Jerry's eyes jerked open. The chair came to the floor with a small crash. "Janet." The voice was mournful and feverish. Scott's eyes were closed and he wore a pained expression. He moaned and his body twitched. "Please wake up, I don't want to bury you." Scott's head moved, his body jerked under the sheet. He moaned again.

Jerry leaned forward watching, his mind racing. What was Scott dreaming about? What was he saying? Bury whom? Scott's face was red and a bead of sweat ran down his neck.

"Under..." He gasped for air. "The palm tree." He moaned softly and collapsed into the pillow, a look of dread on his face.

*****

Scott's eyes opened. The light came into focus. A strange humming sound. A palm tree. A coconut shell to dig with. No, that wasn't where he was. That was a fan he heard. He was... he was... he wasn't sure where he was, actually.

His mind became slowly aware of the pain in his foot and lower waist. He had never seen this place before. Scott jerked up, and looked around. Bare concrete walls, a fan blade beating above him. He had never been here before, he was sure of it. There was someone leaning against the wall in a rusty chair.

"Jerry? Is that you? Where am I?" he demanded. Scott sat up, fearful.

"Calm down. I'm here." Jerry held out a hand to calm him. Scott searched the man's face. Oh, it was Jerry. His mind calmed.

He sank back into the bed, breathing hard. "Jerry, where am I?" He sounded panicky.

"You're at the hospital, remember?" Jerry's voice was soothing. "You woke me up because you were hurting and you passed out when we got to the Henrichs' apartment, Remember? We brought you to the hospital, because you're really sick. That's where you are right now."

Scott relaxed as the information registered. It was all rushing back. Nothing like waking up in a strange room after a nightmare. "I'm thirsty," he croaked. His throat felt dry and hot, his skin was damp.

"Here." Jerry held a cup of water to Scott's lips. "I tried to give you some earlier. You weren't cooperating, though."

Scott drank the whole cup. "I'm cold."

Jerry seemed surprised "You're burning up with a fever, man! It's hot in here."

Scott shook his head. "Have the doctors seen me?"

"No, they should come soon." Jerry looked anxiously toward the door. "There's someone having a baby, and there's only one nurse. I haven't even seen her." He turned back from the door and looked at Scott. "How are you feeling?"

"Not the best, but better with water, at least I'm here at the hospital."

"You'll be fine, man." Jerry stood up, then turned. "What were you talking about just now?"

Scott stared at Jerry blankly. "What do you mean?"

Jerry took one hand from the chair. "You said, don't go, don't go, or something like that, and then something about burying someone under a tree."

Scott's face looked blank for another second, then suddenly changed. "I must have had a nightmare. This fever is doing stuff to me." His tone was defensive.

"It sounded like more than a nightmare to me." Jerry's voice sounded suspicious. "You were talking about Janet. Does that help you remember?"

Scott cringed. His mind whirled. A coconut shell, sand and...no, no, it was fading. He felt his muscles tighten. "No," he said tonelessly.

Jerry looked perplexed. "I'll go get more water." He turned toward the door.

As he exited, he almost ran into a pretty older woman. "I'm so sorry. I'm nurse Kathy." She moved to the side. "There was a woman with a baby, so I couldn't come until right now." She looked like she had been through a long night. "How are you?" She stepped to Scott's bed. "What's your name?"

A few minutes later, she carefully cleaned and bandaged Scott's foot. Jerry stood to the side, watching. Steps approached from the hall, and soon after, the aid came in. She stood for a second, looking at Kathy.

"What can I do?"

Kathy looked up from Scott. "Go get a IV drip ready right away, and get a full 10 CC's of antibiotics." The hospital aid bustled out quickly.

"We'll do what we can for you, Mr. Scott." Kathy gave a tired smile.

"Thank you," Scott replied weakly. "My foot feels better already." His bandaged foot was propped up on the bed frame.

"I'll be back to put the IV in." Kathy disappeared through the door.

Jerry watched her leave, then walked across the floor, head down. He turned to Scott, renewing his questioning. "You were talking about Janet, Scott. I heard you say her name."

Scott looked at him, and his lower lip began to tremble. "I'm scared, Jerry, I don't know what to do."

"What do you mean?" Jerry put his hand on the side of the bed. "Tell me." Scott's mouth opened and closed as he struggled for words.

"Things can't get worse then they are already, Jerry. I'm so confused. I keep having flashbacks of the accident, and every day I remember more. I feel so guilty."

"Why do you feel guilty?" Jerry leaned closer. "If you can trust anyone, you can trust me, Scott." His eyes were sincere. "You need to talk about it."

The room was silent for a second, then Scott began to cry. He slowly recomposed himself.

"I buried her Jerry, but I forgot about it because it was so horrible. When they began looking for her after the wreck, it was like I couldn't remember, so I didn't tell anyone." He began to cry again.

"After the accident, when I swam to the beach, she was dead. I dragged her to shore but it was too late." Scott's voice broke. "I buried her under a palm tree. Now I remember, but I don't know what to do."

"Scott, Scott, it's okay." Jerry's words broke through Scott's mind. "You didn't kill her, she drowned. You did the right thing to bury her." He put a hand on Scott's shoulder. "Don't worry about anything. Just get well, Scott, and I'll take care of this for you."

Scott looked up at Jerry. He looked drained, but relieved to have it off his shoulders.

"I thought you would think I had killed her."

Jerry looked shocked. "Nonsense, it never crossed my mind. I knew something was up, but not like that. You loved Janet more then anybody I knew. I would never think that. Now just relax. It sounds like the nurse is coming back with your IV."

The sound of wheels moving along the hallway increased. "Coming through." The hospital aid pushed the metal rack through the door. "We just called the other nurse. She'll be in to help."

After the aid left, Scott leaned up on his pillow, not satisfied. "Jerry, you can't take care of this. It's my problem, not yours."

"How can you?" retorted Jerry. "All you can to do right now is let go of it, and put your energy into getting well." He was firm. "Everything will be okay."

Scott sighed and let his head fall back. He was too weak to argue.

A new nurse arrived at the hospital a few minutes later. Jerry looked up as she walked into the room.

"I'm Kiera." She stared at Scott for a second, then studied her clipboard. "I'm going to be your nurse. Hmm, it says infection." She looked up and glanced at the IV. "Oh, there it is." She seemed confused. She looked at her papers again, then walked out the door.

Jerry looked at Scott and shrugged. "Not the most friendly."

She returned with a bag. Inside was a yellow plastic cuff, which she tightened around Scott's arm until his veins bulged.

"Hold still." She held up a large needle. "I'm going to start your IV. This might hurt a little bit." Scott let his arm go limp as she held it up. He winced as the needle went in.

"There that's it. You're good." She taped around the insert. "No more sticking you with needles."

Jerry watched, wide-eyed. "I'd be more scared of that needle than the sickness itself. Good job, Scott." He tried to lighten the mood.

Scott laughed nervously from the pillow.

The nurse returned with a syringe. "I'm going to give you your antibiotic now." She connected the syringe with the IV input. "This may hurt a tiny bit." She injected the liquid into the IV. Scott's eyes widened and his arm muscle clinched. "Relax, it's okay," Kiera whispered.

"It feels like battery acid." Scott breathed a short harsh breath. "Oh, that's really painful." He shot a pained glance at the nurse. His muscles tensed.

The nurse continued until the syringe was empty. "There." She held the syringe up to the light. "It's doing its job now." She turned on her heel and walked out.

Scott turned toward Jerry, his eyes watering. "I feel weird. I'm not feeling good now."

Jerry leaned over. "How aren't you feeling good? She just gave you medicine."

"I'm dizzy, and my arm is burning." Scotts voice began to slur and his head slid down onto the pillow. "It's just —" His eyes closed and he fell silent.

"Scott, talk to me, Scott." Jerry grabbed his arm and shook it. "Scott."

Scott made a dim moan. Jerry jumped backwards. For crying out loud! How much could happen in one night? What had the nurse given him? He turned from Scott to the door with two quick steps, then hurried down the hall.

"Nurse, nurse!" Jerry's voice was sharp. "You better come now! My friend is unconscious. His arm was burning after you injected him!"

She looked up defensively from her clipboard. "I just gave him his antibiotic. Is he not responding, or just sleeping?" She looked at Jerry through narrow eyes.

"Yes to the first, no to the second, unless you mean sleeping unconscious." Jerry's voice reflected a touch of anger.

"He was brought in to this hospital unconscious." Kiera consulted her clipboard again. "This is most likely just a relapse." Her tone was sharp, but defensive. She was already walking toward Scott's room.

She looked more worried as she began to examine Scott. He was limp and breathing faintly. His arm was red where she had injected him. "Stay right here, I'll be right back with

Kathy," Kiera commanded. She turned and hurried from the room.

Jerry paced halfway between the door and the bed. Mr. Henrich had said to call him if anything got worse. Should he? He would wait until the nurse got back. He glanced at his watch. 7:30 AM. It had been a roller coaster night. His eyes were tired but fear for his friend kept him awake.

The two nurses came hurrying in. Kathy did a quick examination of Scott, then began to say something, changed her mind, then pulled Kiera into the hallway.

"Please stay here." She spoke to Jerry in a no nonsense tone.

Jerry stopped and stood still. Why did she say that? He cocked his ear. He could hear muffled voices in the hallway, rising and falling. Only a few words were distinct. "You didn't dilute …antibiotics? Direct injection?" He could hear the younger nurse's plaintive tone. That was it. Jerry stepped out into the hall. They had given Scott something bad. He knew that much. It was time to explain.

The two nurses stopped abruptly and turned toward him. "I asked you to stay-"

"No! You need to explain!" Jerry cut the nurse off in mid-sentence. "What did you give him? I have to know. I'm going to call Director Henrich right now. His wife is a nurse and she'll be arriving shortly." Jerry let his sentence tumble out.

The nurses exchanged glances, then Kathy spoke. "We made a mistake. We didn't dilute the antibiotic before we injected him. Normally it takes 100 cc's of solution to 10 mgs of antibiotic. We are sorry, but we don't know what his reaction will be." She took a deep breath.

"Well, so far it seems really BAD!"

The younger nurse shrank back.

"Getting upset will help no one." Kathy's voice was even. She stepped forward firmly. "You need to get control of yourself, otherwise I'm going to ask you to leave. We need clear thinking right now."

Jerry stopped himself and stood shaking. "What should I tell Henrich?" he muttered.

"Tell him that Scott's unconscious, and ask if his wife knows anything about this drug's overdose effects, and stay calm." Kathy looked from Jerry to Kiera. "We will give him the dilute solution, and monitor him closely."

"After that, I think you need to go home and rest," she said. "You're exhausted, Jerry."

Jerry looked back at her. "I'll stay calm. I'm no more tired than you. I'm going to stay with my friend."

Before she could stop him Jerry turned and hurried down the hall. He picked up the phone and punched in the number. It rang twice.

"Hello? Henrich speaking..."

"Hi, it's Jerry." He leaned on the counter, stopping to collect himself. "Scott is worse. They gave him an antibiotic that wasn't diluted properly, and he's unconscious. Can your wife help?"

The line crackled. "Why didn't you call sooner?" Henrich's voice became audibly upset.

"It just happened right now. Before he was fine, we were talking and everything," Jerry said defensively.

"Okay then, we're on the way out the door," Henrich said.

Jerry heard the phone click and the disconnected beeping. He set the phone down. What should he do? An idea came to his brain. Maybe he was delusional, maybe not. Charcoal. His tired mind grasped at the idea.

That would help Scott. He turned from the phone and walked toward the hospital exit, through the door, and out into the sunny street.

Only a few very high clouds floated in the salty breeze. The dawn did not reflect the past night's chaos.

Where could he find charcoal? Jerry's brain raced around the island. The store wouldn't be open yet. Not the school. What about the hospital he had just exited? He paused. Best not to bother the nurses again after his outburst. Only one place left. There would be some charcoal in the teachers' dormitory.

Jerry hurried down the street and around the corner. He arrived at the apartment out of breath. He took the side stairs three at a time. Knocking on the door, he heard no answer. He turned the knob, stepped inside, and quickly began looking through the kitchen cupboard. Jerry didn't notice the man sitting on the couch.

"What are you looking for?"

Jerry turned. Someone with a bandage on his head was sitting on the couch. "Tony?" Jerry stared. "I'm looking for charcoal. Scott's in the hospital down the street, and he's unconscious."

"He's in the hospital?" Tony was surprised. "From what?"

"An infection from a cut on his foot."

They hadn't seen each other since Scott and Tony's incident.

"Oh," Tony said. "The charcoal is in that drawer." He pointed. "Help yourself."

Jerry returned to the hospital and hurried to Scott's room. The Henrichs were already there and only glanced up as Jerry walked in. Kathy was adjusting the IV.

"When will the doctor be in?" Mr. Henrich stood popping his knuckles.

"He's due on the morning boat," Kathy said. "Any time." She leaned over Scott, listening to his lungs. She was worried.

The younger nurse came into the room. She looked pale. "I called the pharmacist from Quadraline. He said that unconsciousness and kidney failure could result. All we can do is wait and keep him well hydrated." She glanced from face to face.

Mr. Henrich let out a deep breath. "That's just great."

Jerry saw his opportunity. "Mr. Henrich, everyone. Charcoal will help absorb the infection from the wound, and also any harmful substances. I have some here." He held up his bottle. The Henrichs and the two nurses turned toward him, skeptical.

Elizabeth reached out and took the bottle. "It's worth a try, there's nothing else we can do." She turned to Kiera. "Lets mix it with water so he can drink it, and prepare a poultice for his foot."

Jerry watched as the nurses made a poultice and pressed it gently onto the angry red wound and then pumped black charcoal paste down Scott's throat.

Mr. Henrich watched in silence. "I'm glad to see he's in good hands. All we can do is wait now." He turned. "I will go call the district president. I'm sure he'll want to know about this situation." He paused and looked at Jerry. "I'll stop by the dorm and tell Scott's friends, just in case." He gave Jerry a meaningful glance. "Jerry, you can supervise any visitors who come."

Time passed. Jerry sat on his chair. The nurses came in at regular intervals to check on their patient. Several students from the mission came in to see Scott. They stood in solemn huddles, watching. Some prayed, while others just stared wide-eyed. The whole room was quiet, almost reverent.

Some older Christian islanders also came. They talked in hushed tones and prayed. A few cried. Jerry sat motionless, watching through it all. He answered the questions people asked, but otherwise remained quiet.

The room was finally empty. The nurse had left. Jerry sat quietly on the chair, watching the rising and falling of Scott's chest.

Someone coughed. Jerry looked up. Tony stood silhouetted in the door. He still had the bandage on his head. He looked towards Scott's still form. He glanced toward Jerry. His eyes were sincere and pleading.

"Could I have just a minute with him?" He paused. "Alone?" His voice was humble and he spoke in a respectful tone, unusual from the normal arrogant Tony.

Jerry rose from his chair. "I'll stand outside." He nodded at Tony.

Tony looked down. "Thank you."

Jerry walked out into the hall and leaned against the wall. He could hear Tony step toward the bed and speak.

"Scott, I'm so sorry, I need to tell you." Tony's voice was full of emotion. "You saved my life, you were right to hit me with that chair. I'm sorry for being so arrogant and not listening. I'm sorry about Janet, too. I'm sorry it took me so long to realize it."

Jerry heard the chair squeak and Tony appeared in the door. He wiped a tear from his eye and looked away.

"Thank you." His voice was husky. "I need to go." He started walking, then stopped and turned. "Jerry. You've always been a true friend to Scott, much better than me." He nodded, then turned and retreated with rapid steps.

Two hours later the doctor arrived. He was a busy man who supervised six different island hospitals and clinics. He listened to Scott's lungs while everyone watched.

"It sounds like fluid is collecting." He replaced his stethoscope around his neck. "I'm sure you have contacted his next of kin. All we can do is pray, it's all in God's hands. Good idea with the charcoal, Elizabeth. I just hope it wasn't too late." The doctor nodded toward her.

She had called the doctor an hour before and had given him a heavy explanation of Scott's condition.

Jerry sat silently in his chair. It didn't matter that the charcoal was his idea. Only one thing mattered. "God, please help Scott make it through the night."

Chapter 3

The air was heavy, Scott felt himself struggling to breathe. He knew he must be in the hospital because he heard the nurse above him somewhere. Why was he trying so hard? Scott began to relax, he let his muscles loosen and he felt himself sinking into the bed. Everything was so peaceful, so quiet.

The light behind his eyelids swam back and forth, getting darker. It was a dark room to a tired traveler, appealing to his exhaustion. He felt the picture envelope him, dark fuzzy blackness. It was so comfortable, he liked it. He felt warm. Faint at first, a small white spot came out of the darkness. It seemed to expand and push the blackness away. The white-gray mist kept growing until it surrounded Scott. He felt letdown. He could feel that something was meant to happen. He looked around and saw ground below him. He felt himself standing and walking. It was foggy.

Scott looked down at his feet. No pain. He shook his arm, no IV. Scott felt energy surging in his veins. He strode along, feeling good. Breathing was easy! He looked around. It was cloudy, but the clouds were lifting. A beam of sun shot through the mist. Hills became visible, dark and indistinct at first, but clearing as the mist lifted. The hills were covered in rich green vegetation. Scott turned his head, his eyes drinking in his dream-like surroundings. He was walking along a dirt road in a valley, the hills on all sides of him growing larger in the distance. A river ran on the right of the road, and willows and cottonwood grew around the banks. It was still misty, but the temperature was rising. The sun shone onto Scott's back. As he walked forward, birds chirped, a gentle breeze rustled through the cottonwoods. He could see large outcroppings of rock jutting from among the trees on the hill. As he walked, the road got bigger. There was a large group of trees ahead. He could see people standing around, some with their hands in their pockets, others talking on cell phones. They all seemed to be waiting. As he advanced, Scott could see picnic tables. There were a lot of people, but no one appeared to be doing anything. Oh, there was at least some activity. Scott looked out across the grass, almost like a park. Children were running and playing.

As Scott walked onto the grass, a tall man with piercing, dark eyes looked up from where he was typing on a slim laptop. He was the only one sitting at the tables. He looked very distinguished, and was very well dressed. Over six feet tall, with jet black hair combed impeccably back across his head, along with a quaint little ponytail.

He gazed at Scott, stood and walked energetically across the grass toward him. His face was smooth with a prominent nose, and a thin forehead. He reached a muscular arm out and pumped Scott's hand in a firm handshake. "I see you're new here, let me show you around." His accent was rich and deep. A tingle went up Scott's spine. He could feel the man's incredible energy. With one large arm, he reached around Scott in a friendly but overpowering gesture. He turned Scott towards the road. "The people by the trees don't have a clue." The man sounded so confident, so much smarter.

"Yes," Scott sputtered. He felt compelled to agree with this man. "Why are they just standing there?" He felt like a small child being pulled by a large uncle. He looked up timidly.

The man threw back his head and laughed; a deep, bubbling laugh. "Ohhhh, hahaha, you mean you don't know?"

Scott squirmed. He felt stupid. "Uh, no." He looked down. Strange. Should he know?

The man pulled Scott closer with his bulging biceps, and spoke in a conspiring whisper. "It's because they don't know what I know." He looked down charismatically. "Oh, don't feel bad, it's my secret." He pulled Scott forward. "That's why I wait at the park. I've seen many, many people come through there." He loosened his hold on Scott now that they were walking along the road. "When I saw you, I instantly knew you were better. So young, and obviously very smart." He smiled at Scott. "I pick the brightest and best first."

Scott felt uncomfortable. He didn't want to seem stupid. "Thanks, I'm honored."

The man looked at him, bemused. "Honored?" He laughed. "Oh no..." His voice was playful but firm. "You got it all wrong. You deserve this, it's yours by right." He patted Scott on the back. "You have a lot to learn, but you'll do."

Scott looked up at the man wonderingly. "What's your name?"

"What's my name?" He sounded dumbfounded, then chuckled. "You want to know a secret?" Scott nodded. "I haven't been asked that question in a long time, not many people ask." He winked. "Once I show them what I have, they forget all about me and become obsessed." He held up his hand, "Not that that's bad, of course, but it is nice to get noticed from time to time."

"So what's your name?" Scott asked again.

"Well, what do you think my name is?" He peered at Scott, eyes twinkling. "Should I guess your name?"

"Try," said Scott frustrated. "If you can't guess it the first time, then you have to tell me your name."

"Okay then," the man muttered. "Very demanding, but that's good." His voice trailed off. "Well, let me think." He seemed to be enjoying himself. He twisted his head suddenly. "It's Scott."

Scott felt shocked. How in the world did this man know his name? He was sure he'd never seen him before.

The man grinned. "Lucky guess?"

"No, that's my name!" Scott said, bewildered. "Do you know me?"

"Maybe yes, maybe no. Like I said, lucky guess." The man was very intriguing.

"What's your name?" Scott demanded.

The man cocked his head so his dark hair fell forward. "Oh, but I don't have to tell you. I guessed your name, now you need to guess mine." His voice was rich.

"But I couldn't possibly know," protested Scott.

"You can call me whatever you want. How's that?" The tall stranger smiled. "Teacher would be good, because you have much to learn."

Scott felt subdued. "Okay, Teacher."

"That's good, that's good!" The man couldn't hide his grin. "Let me show you what you can have!"

"Okay," Scott said.

Ahead were two roads. One was smoother and swung gradually to the left. A group of bicyclists sailed by smoothly down that road. One man in a biking suit raised a hand and smiled as he passed.

"Beautiful day." And then he was gone, speeding away.

Scott continued to look around. To the right, another road went up alongside the mountain and disappeared behind some trees. Scott could see it going up the side of the mountain.

"Aww, Don't look at that road," the Teacher muttered. "Wrong road." He pointed down the road the bikers had sailed. "Look there."

Scott strained his ears. He could hear honking, and he could smell engine exhaust coming up from the valley.

"Come this way." The Teacher beckoned. He led Scott out between where the road split, and helped Scott climb a large boulder that lay between the junction. From on top, Scott could see both roads much better, the road going up the mountain on his right, and the paved road going down into a valley on his left. He saw brake lights on the left for what seemed like miles and miles and could hear motorists honking. A thin haze of smog hung over the huge traffic jam.

"Want a better look?" The Teacher smiled and held out a pair of binoculars. Scott took them and looked down at the traffic jam. He could see a man standing on his van roof, looking down the road, trying to figure out where the traffic jam ended. Scott thought he looked stressed and frustrated. He also saw the same bikers from earlier walking their bicycles along the side of the road. "Don't look at the road, look ahead." The Teacher reached out and bumped the binoculars with a long finger.

Scott moved his eyes where directed and saw distant high-rise buildings through the haze. He strained to see, "Is that smog? I can't see." He put the binoculars down. "Why is there such a huge traffic jam? I don't think I like that road."

The Teacher laughed and swung his ponytail with a whoosh. "Just goes to show you how popular the road is! You would like that road, especially since I can get you in the fast lane." He pointed. "See, to the far left." He pushed the binoculars to Scott. "Take another look."

Scott lifted the binoculars again. He could see an empty lane to the far left. It was barricaded off with a concrete wall, with guards armed with rifles standing by its only gate. Some people were looking wishfully over the wall from their cars in the traffic jam.

"That's my V.I.P. lane." The Teacher puffed out his chest. "I found that my highway was so popular that I had to get a lane made just for me and my friends, because traffic is such a drag. So many people go down this highway that it would be bumper to bumper and near impossible without being in that lane." The Teacher pointed. "Watch the gate now."

Scott peered through the binoculars. A green Porsche with a young blonde in it drove up to the gate. A guard walked to her car. She reached out and handed him a small black card. He swiped it in a reader and the gate opened. She drove through and accelerated down the empty lane, passing hundreds of stopped cars in seconds.

"You see, only those with my access key can get in that lane." The Teacher turned to Scott. "I might consider offering you one." He paused and reached inside his leather jacket, pulling out a thin stack of black cards. With a poker player's flair, he counted them in his long fingers. He raised his eyebrows. "It depends." He leaned back against the rock, smiling when he saw Scott look with longing at the black cards. He slid them back into his jacket. "What are you interested in?" His voice held an edge of mystery. "Girls? Or lots of girls perhaps?" He smiled knowingly. "Money?" He reached inside his jacket again and this time pulled out a fat roll of large bills. "I'm an easy-going guy." He stretched. "Thinking about what I said earlier, I think I was wrong." He smiled benignly. "I think you are honored." His eyes were large as they bore into Scott. He glanced over his shoulder, almost with a hint of anxiety. "Lets get you down to the road and get you hooked up then, shall we?"

Scott began to nod. The big man reached, took him by the arm, and began walking toward the road, dragging Scott with him. He seemed to be in a rush.

All of a sudden, a man was on their right. He radiated a pleasant confidence. Scott turned his head from under the Teacher's shoulder and gazed toward him, looking at his deep brown eyes.

The Teacher grew agitated. "Come on now." He pulled on Scott's arm. "We've no time to waste."

The man on the right touched Scott on the shoulder. Scott turned, forcing the Teacher to stop.

"He's not interested!" the teacher barked.

The man stood his ground. "I haven't heard him say that," he responded solidly.

He was also tall, and wore elegant yet simple clothing, quite a contrast to the gaudy black leather that hung from the Teacher's shoulders.

"Tell him you're not interested," the Teacher commanded.

The other man stepped forward. "Let Scott find out himself, you know the rules."

The Teacher let go of Scott's shoulders grudgingly. "Make it quick," he hissed at Scott sharply. "My time is limited, and I have few black cards."

"My name is Michael," the man said. "Were you told there was another road?" He looked concerned.

Scott was confused. "I saw another road, but no, I haven't been shown it." He twisted to look at the Teacher.

"Do you know how hard it is? As opposed to my road?" the Teacher retorted.

"Have you shown him the end of your road? As opposed to my road?" Michael responded. "Or was it hidden in the smog?"

The Teacher shrank back. "Unfair!" he spat. The Teacher looked at Scott. His face seemed to convey pity, but it made Scott's hair stand on end. "I can guarantee you that you will have no fun if you follow that road." His eyes became silky black. "I can guarantee I have your best interest at heart. I want you to have fun!"

"Fun or true joy?" Michael stepped forward, "Tell him the truth." His voice was firm.

"Fun," muttered the Teacher, stepping back again.

Scott stood between the two. He looked back and forth between the Teacher and Michael. The Teacher stood, chest heaving. His leather jacket hung from his frame and large rings covered his clinched fist. He unclenched when he saw Scott looking. Scott turned back to Michael, who stood solid. His eyes hid nothing and his hands were open.

"What is true happiness anyways? You've never even known true happiness. Is it even real? Go with what you know, Scott." The Teacher's voice was persuasive.

Scott looked back at Michael.

"Look to me," said Michael.

Scott stood for a second. Why hadn't the Teacher shown him anything about the other way? There was something about him that made Scott feel very uncomfortable. But then again, he hadn't seen Michael show any VIP lane or talk of girls.

He turned back toward the Teacher. "I'm going to go with Michael. You do not want to tell me where your road ends, so I don't want to go on it."

The Teacher turned, a look of hate on his face. "Okay, you ungrateful rat," he snarled. He reached into his jacket and flung a black card to the ground, stomping on it with his black boot. "I can see I was wrong, you are very stupid, with no regard to your future. I have no time to waste on someone like you." He turned and walked furiously away.

Scott and Michael stood in the road, watching the retreating figure.

"I'm very happy you listened." Michael stepped back. "You will be able to see for yourself where his road goes."

Scott watched the Teacher disappear in the direction of the park.

"Are you ready to see the other road?"

Scott nodded. "I'm just a little shaken up, but I think I'm ready."

"If you need to rest, we can." Michael pointed to a smooth mound of grass at the bottom of the mountain road. "That's a good spot, out of the road."

He looked at the road he was standing in. "I haven't seen any traffic."

Michael shook his head. "The Teacher kept it clean while he showed you his road, but now this is not a safe place for you to be." He led the way to the small grassy knoll. Scott followed behind. Just then he heard a screeching sound. As he looked back toward the road, an eighteen-wheeler hurtled around the road and sped down into the valley.

The two began to walk up the road. Scott looked around at the hillside, which only seemed to ascend. On one side of this road was a deep precipice, and the other was a high hill, which turned into a high, rocky cliff as Scott and Michael progressed. Scott gazed down the side of the mountain. He could see the valley far below, and the distant haze from the freeway. Scott pointed. "I still can't see where that road goes, all I can see is a lot of haze and a few big buildings."

Michael was quiet. His eyes swept across the panoramic view. "You'll understand." He paused. "Soon." He turned up the trail. "I have someone I want you to meet."

Up ahead, a red truck was parked on a dirt pullout. The truck looked familiar to Scott. Where had he seen it before? Scott began to remember. It was his uncle Matthew's truck! The truck he had learned to drive in when he was a teenager. That Ford held a lot of memories. Scott remembered riding to work with Matthew in it. Of course, that was all before his uncle's death. He hadn't seen the truck since he left Alaska, but here it was, parked in front of him.

Scott ran up toward the truck. He banged on its side. "Uncle Matthew! Uncle Matthew!"

The door to the cab swung open. Matthew sprang out and caught Scott in a big bear hug. For a second he squeezed him, then held Scott out at arm's length and surveyed him. "So good to see you." He wiped his eye. "You've grown into quite a man."

Scott stared back at his uncle. Red beard, blue eyes, big beefy frame. The top of his plaid shirt was un-buttoned, showing a glimpse of his hairy chest. Same Carrhart pants, even down to the steel-toed boots. His uncle hadn't changed a bit.

"There's someone else you should meet, I'll reckon she's a tad more pretty then your old uncle." Matthew chuckled. He turned Scott back toward the truck. A young woman stepped out of the truck. She looked at Scott and smiled.

"Janet?" Scott gasped. He stumbled forward. They caught each other in an embrace. Her brownish-gold hair brushed against his cheeks. Her brown eyes glowed.

"Hi, Scott."

Scott stood in a happy daze. He hadn't seen these people for so long. It was so wonderful being with Janet again. A wall of feelings had been unlocked inside of him. He hadn't felt so good for a long time. It was good, very good to feel love again.

"We need to start driving. We can get reacquainted on the road." Matthew was smiling. "Why don't you, Michael and Janet ride in the back, and I'll drive my truck."

A minute later the truck began to bounce up the road. In the back, Scott clutched the side, squinting through the wind down into the valley. Janet was next to him, her hair blowing, and Michael sat across from them.

"What a strange freeway," Scott mused.

Janet looked where Scott was pointing. "It shouldn't be called a 'Freeway,'" she said. "A toll road is more like it, and the price cannot be any higher."

Michael spoke. "Can you see, Scott, more of where that road ends?"

Scott peered over the side of the truck. He could see a dark gorge. He looked away. It made him dizzy, it was so far below. As the truck continued to climb, Scott kept glancing over the side.

"The road is getting more narrow. What if it gives way?" Scott looked at Michael with fear in his eyes. Janet glanced apprehensively over the cliff. The truck's tires were inches from the edge, advancing forward at a crawl.

The cliff's edge fell hundreds and hundreds of feet to the gorge far below. The truck stopped and Scott felt the truck shudder as Matthew set the E-brake. He shut the engine off and left the keys dangling in the ignition. Scott watched him crawl across the seat. He couldn't get out on his side without jumping off the cliff.

"The road is too narrow. We need to walk from here," said his uncle as he squeezed between the door and the rock. "I can't drive any further without rolling off the cliff."

He reached back inside the cab and tugged a backpack and water bottle out. "Carry some water and a jacket." He tossed Scott a windbreaker. "Stay close to the wall, the other side is crumbling away."

The four started walking away from the truck. Clinging close to the cliff side, a stiff breeze pelted them with small pieces of sand. Scott shivered even with his coat. If he didn't trust Michael and his uncle, he was sure he would have turned back. It was getting foggy ahead. Scott glanced at Janet, who seemed calm and focused, her attention directed to the path ahead. Just watching her calmness slowed his thumping pulse. If she wasn't afraid, then he shouldn't be either. Scott looked back up the trail. Through the fog, two figures moved toward them, and they passed by quickly, without even looking up to acknowledge them.

After they passed, Scott climbed up to his uncle. "What if they take the truck?" he asked in a low voice. "You left the keys in the ignition."

His uncle took a deep breath. "I don't need it anymore. It's all right Scott. We can't use it up here."

Scott tugged at his uncle's sleeve. "Why do we have to leave so much behind?" He paused. "Why continue up this road?" He looked at his uncle, his eyes full of questions and fear.

"Why wouldn't we go up this path?" Matthew acted like Scott was asking him a silly question, "It's the only path worth taking. It goes somewhere I want to be." His uncle spoke with longing in his voice. "Come on, stay close." He turned and continued on the trail ahead.

Scott followed in silence, deep in thought. An abrupt noise from below echoed up the mountain. The sound of a diesel engine starting a few thousand feet below. "They're taking your truck," Scott hissed. "What should we do?"

Michael held up a hand. "Quiet." The four stood listening, the rumbling engine revved and Scott could hear a popping sound as the E-brake released. It sounded like the truck was moving away from them. The horn's distinctive honk rattled up the mountain, a sliding sound, and then a loud bang. Scott stepped toward the side to look.

His uncle caught him by the shirt. "Careful."

Scott leaned forward. A thundering sound continued to echo. He could see the red truck tumbling like a broken tin can down the side of the mountain, a cloud of dust rolling behind it. It banged and splintered until it came to rest below by a large boulder. An eerie silence replaced the thundering fall. Scott stood shocked. The truck had just slid off the cliff. The group stood in hushed stillness, looking at each other. Matthew turned with Michael and began to walk.

"Come on, Scott, we must go." Janet tugged at Scott's arm. "We can't stop for anything now."

Scott nodded. "Okay." He followed Janet, just looking over his shoulder once. This time he couldn't see behind him anymore, the fog was too thick.

As they continued, the path became narrower and narrower, until the group was forced to lean against the rock wall for balance. Once Scott hit his toe on a small loose rock. Several seconds later he heard it make a slight "dink" far below.

"Careful" murmured Janet. She glanced back at him.

From far below, the sounds of a carnival drifted to Scott's ears. He could hear raucous voices making vulgar jokes, and several low, heavy beats. There was laughter, mingled with cursing and cries of bitter disappointment. It made Scott more anxious to stay on the narrow, difficult trail.

Along the wall, red cords appeared. They hung to Scott's waist height, swaying in the air.

"Hold on to the cords," shouted Matthew "They'll be able to hold your weight."

Scott watched Janet walk in front of him. She held the cords as she inched her way up the trail. Scott looked at a cord, and tugged at it. He wasn't sure it would hold him. He kept leaning against the cliff and inching forward.

"Scott." Janet turned to look at him. "You have to hold on to the cords, otherwise you'll fall. They'll hold your weight just like they've held those who've gone before us."

Scott nodded. He grasped the cord in his hands and gave a tug. His stomach turned. The cord held. Through the fog, Scott could only hear her voice. Only Janet's back was visible now, against the edge of the wall. He loosened his water bottle from his belt and took one last chugging gulp before he tossed it into the fog. As the group began its final ascent, Scott felt his feet slipping on the edge of the path. An icy fear gripped him. He grasped a red cord, thinking he would fall, but then he didn't. The cord held.

Up ahead the fog began to clear. Scott could see a chasm. It was like the trail ended on the edge of a great canyon.

"What now?" Scott yelled shakily. The rock wall was ending, and on all other sides he could not see past the dark clouds below.

"Hold on to the red cord," yelled Matthew. "You'll fall if you don't."

About forty feet across the chasm was a plateau. It was green and there was no fog. It looked bright and safe.

"We have to swing across." yelled Matthew. "Follow me." He wrapped his cord around his wrist and looked back into Scott's eyes for a second.

Scott saw no fear. With as much spring as he could manage, Matthew leaped from the cliff side. Scott watched in fascinated horror. Then Matthew sailed over the canyon and fell into the grass. He rolled over and waved. "It works!" he yelled.

Janet gripped her cord. "You'll be right behind me, Scott, right?" She looked at Scott.

"Yes." He nodded "I'll be right behind you."

Janet took a deep breath and launched herself away. A few seconds later, she had swung to safety. Matthew grabbed her as she swung past him and the two fell into the grass. Scott gripped his cord, feeling dizzy. He looked down. He could see the sides of the cliff disappearing into darkness. He felt sick. He jerked the cord. It felt loose.

"What's it secured to?" He shook as he spoke. He turned to Michael.

"It will not fail." Michael put a firm hand on Scott. "The cord is attached to a rock that cannot be moved. Just hold onto it. I have a work for you that you cannot do yourself."

Scott stood, sweating profusely, by the edge of the cliff. He had never felt so frightened before.

"Are you coming?" Janet called from across the cliff. Scott looked across. She was waving from the grass. "Trust the cord please, Scott."

Scott wrapped the cord around his wrist. It felt so flimsy, but there was no other way. He closed his eyes for a second, then leaped. His legs shook as they left the ground. He felt his heart pound in his throat. He was falling, no, swinging, into the chasm. The air whistled around him with a chilling sound. He opened his eyes and the wind made tears come.

He wasn't swinging up. Scott felt disappointment so keen it made his body ache. He was swinging into the cloud and he felt himself lowering. No! No! NO! He wanted to be on the plateau with Janet and Matthew.

He kicked his legs. *Go up. Go up,* his mind frantically screamed. He pulled on the cord. It was unwrapping. Why wasn't it holding him up?

Chapter 4

"Scott." A voice entered the fog. "Scott. Stop trying to twist your IV around your arm, it will come out!"

Scott's eyes opened. A nurse was above him, tugging at his arm. He felt his legs, heavy in the tangled blankets. Cold sweat ran down Scott's forehead. He lay unmoving, his wits coming back to him. There it was, that familiar pain in his foot.

"Where's Jerry?" Scott asked.

"He went out. He said he'd be back this morning." The nurse was readjusting Scott's IV. "I'm glad you're awake. You've been improving since about three this morning. Are you hungry?"

Scott shook his head no. "What happened?"

"You got sick from a medicine, dear, but you're improving now."

Scott leaned back on his pillow and bit his lip. He was so angry. Janet was fresh in his mind now. It was all like a fresh wound had been sliced across the old one. "I wish I hadn't woken up." Scott spoke in a groggy voice.

"Oh, don't talk like that, you're just a young man, and you're getting stronger by the hour," said Kathy. She was straightening the blankets on the bed. "Now that you're awake, try not to kick the blankets off."

Scott grimaced inside. Her voice was like an annoying bee sting of reality. "Sorry," he mumbled. He rolled over halfway.

"Careful with your IV, dear. I'll be back with your breakfast."

Scott began to sit up. "I'm not hungry."

She was already gone. He sighed and settled back down.

Scott watched a fly buzz around the ceiling. It made a low buzzing sound that almost matched the pounding in his head. A minute later he heard footsteps returning.

"I brought you some milk, and a banana." Nurse Kathy set the tray next to the bed. "Let me help you sit up, and see if you can eat." She propped a pillow so Scott could sit up. "Mr. Henrich will be here soon." She brought the banana up to Scott's lips.

He felt awkward. "I haven't had someone feed me for a long time." Milk dribbled down his chin when she held the cup to his lips.

"This will help you regain your strength so you can feed yourself. You haven't eaten for the two days you've been here." Kathy smiled.

Scott took one last bite of banana and shook his head. "Too much," he said through a mouthful.

"This won't be the last time you'll be fed by a lady." Kathy was trying to cheer Scott.

"Why?" Scott mumbled.

"You're a young man. You still need a girl in a white dress to feed you cake. The girls will be all over you back in the States." Kathy smirked.

She had made a mistake. Scott's face changed and he clenched up. "I'm not leaving the Islands," he said stiffly. "I don't want to see any girls."

Kathy tried to be soothing. "There, there, I was trying to joke."

Just then the door opened and Mr. Henrich stuck his head in. "Hi, Scott. I see you're eating breakfast. I hope you'll be feeling well enough to travel soon."

Scott looked up from his milk, alarmed. "Travel?"

The nurse glanced worriedly at Scott and then back to Mr. Henrich. She shook her head.

Mr. Henrich saw her look and hesitated, but then continued.

"I have a ticket made for you to leave Thursday morning."

Scott didn't notice that the milk in his hand was spilling on the sheets. He stared back at Mr. Henrich uncomprehending, shock and dismay on his face.

"Why?" Scott finally blurted.

"I'm sorry for being so blunt." Mr. Henrich stepped to the bed and laid a hand on Scott's shoulder. "Son, our board of directors voted on it yesterday." He paused. "Because of what happened between you and Tony, since you were the aggressor…" He let his words trail off. "It influenced the decision. And you're in the hospital. If we lose another faculty member by violence or disease, we'll be shut down. They already think we are careless with the student missionaries."

"But, but I'm getting better," Scott protested. "See, I'm eating and I can be back to teaching in days." He looked pleading at Mr. Henrich. "And I've already explained what happened with Tony, don't you believe me? Please, can we appeal to the board?"

Mr. Henrich shook his head. "Scott, I know you love these islands, but you are still very sick, we don't have the medical facilities to give you the care you need." He cleared his throat.

"The decision is final, I've already made a ticket to Guam. I arranged with your uncle there. They have a first rate hospital that can handle any complications you may have. From there, you can arrange to fly back to the States."

Scott looked shocked, "I—" He looked away. "How soon?"

"Today's Tuesday," Mr. Henrich answered. "You'll need to be ready by 2 PM Thursday. I stopped by the dorm and told Jerry, he'll help you pack your things."

Scott slumped onto the pillow, his appetite gone. "I can't eat anymore." He pushed the milk away from himself.

"I'll be stopping by to pick you up this afternoon." Mr. Henrich patted Scott's arm. "I'll take you to the dorm, you can rest and pack there."

Scott watched him leave in silence. He felt miserable, like his entire life had just crashed in two stupid slips. If he'd just let Tony get what he deserved, and not gone shark fishing...

Kathy left the room with the tray. Scott buried his head in the pillow, and then the tears came, tears of bitter frustration, fear, and pain. He sobbed into the pillow. He didn't want to leave the Marshall Islands. They were the best place he had known. And now it was ending.

"Scott?" Jerry's voice was tentative. "Are you okay?" He let the door swing shut behind him.

Scott looked up tearfully from his pillow. He wiped his free hand across his face. "I'll be fine," he muttered. "Mr. Henrich just stopped by and told me I have to leave." Scott's voice quaked.

"I'm just glad you made it after that antibiotic." Jerry walked across the room.

"Yes, but I have to leave now," Scott repeated, despondent.

Jerry's face showed the anger he felt. He took a deep breath. "Not for two more days, you don't. Let's get you out of this hospital, so you can enjoy them."

Nurse Kathy's footsteps approached, "Oh, hi, Jerry." She walked back in and smiled. She walked over to Scott. "I'm going to take your IV out. You don't need it anymore." She unwrapped the tape from his arm and removed the IV with a slow tug. "There." She held a cotton pad over the spot, rewrapping it in medical tape.

Kathy helped Scott sit up on the pillow. Jerry helped him swing his legs to the side of the bed. "Careful with your foot," Jerry warned. Scott nodded.

"Henrich is coming back with his truck," Kathy said. "Aren't you happy to go home?"

Scott didn't say anything. He was too upset to respond.

*****

Mr. Henrich helped Scott climb the steps to the apartment. "We'll see you in a little while, Scott." He turned and started down the stairs. "You let us know if you need anything."

Scott nodded. "Okay, thanks Mr. Henrich." He limped into the apartment and sat down on the couch. "Jerry," Scott called. "I'm going to take a shower. I might be a while. If you need anything, yell."

Jerry walked in carrying Scott's bag, "If you need help, I'll be in the living room, okay?"

Scott limped to the bathroom and closed the door. He undressed and stepped into the shower. The shower was like his own world. Once he shut the curtain, everything was somewhere else. It was just him and the flowing hot water.

Why did this happen? Scott stared at the tiled wall. Why did he have to leave? He still couldn't believe it. His mind was whirling, trying to catch up. The water made a dim splattering sound against the tub. Scott looked up, angry. "God." He slapped the tub. "Why?" He thumped his head against the side, moaning. "I don't understand," he muttered.

"Everything okay in there?" a voice called through the bathroom door.

Scott lifted his head. "I'm fine, Jerry."

"Just checking. I'm going to turn the fan on, it's all steamed up in here." Jerry shut the door.

Scott leaned back in the shower. He closed his eyes. He didn't want to think about anything.

Twenty minutes later, Scott opened the bathroom door. A cloud of steam escaped as he limped to the bedroom, towel around his waist.

"Hey Scott, you know what we talked about in the hospital, about Janet?" Jerry walked in behind him.

Scott groaned and pulled a shirt over his head. "Yeah?"

"Janet's dad arrived here on Ebi this morning. He just came in from the airport on Quadraline, where he was managing the search for his daughter. I talked with him by phone yesterday. He wants to talk with you."

"You mean he's here on Ebi to talk with me?" Scott stepped out of the bedroom, buttoning up his shorts. He looked pale.

"Yes." Jerry nodded. "He canceled his search airplane to come here."

It felt like a hammer had hit Scott in the side. He felt fear forming again. He forced himself to breath. "I better talk to him about it." He looked at Jerry. "Where can I find him?"

"He's most likely at the school office. I'll help you find him." Jerry held up the bandages from Nurse Kathy. "Bandage your foot first, and wear your tennis shoes so it doesn't get dirty."

Scott nodded and reached for the bandage. He'd learned the hard way that it paid to keep a wound clean. "I haven't worn my tennis shoes in months."

The two made their way out of the apartment and down the steps. The tennis shoes felt strange and constricting on Scott's feet. He was used to wearing sandals, or going barefoot.

"Why don't you wait on beach, Scott?" Jerry turned to Scott as they neared the school office. "That would be a good place to talk with her dad. I'll run up to the office and find him."

Scott hobbled down to the shore and waited, breathless. He felt like an old man having to hobble around and rest so often. He propped his foot up. His heel was sore and the bandage made the shoe uncomfortably tight. He looked up toward the school office. No one was visible. What was taking Jerry so long?

Scott rehearsed what he would tell Janet's dad over and over in his mind. At least Jerry had talked to him earlier. Scott had never met any of Janet's family before, but he imagined a large man, probably over six feet, with deep blue eyes and a face just like Janet's. The thought of her made his lower lip tremble. He was still in love. In his mind, he could imagine her dad's response. "You what? Buried her under a palm tree?" And then a large man attacking him with both fists flying. Scott shivered, and shook the image from his head.

"Stay calm," he told himself. "I did the right thing."

He was brought to reality by footsteps in the sand. He looked up. A thin man who was shorter then Janet was walking down the path. Scott saw his eyes. Brown eyes, and a thin gray hairline. *This can't be Janet's dad*, Scott thought. *He doesn't look anything close to her.* Scott looked again. Perhaps the nose?

"Hi." The man spoke. "Jerry said you wanted to speak with me." He reached out and shook Scott's hand. "My name's William. You must be Scott." His face was calm, but his eyes looked soulful and a little red.

"You're Janet's dad?" Scott asked with uncertainty.

"Yes, I am," William said. "You looking for someone else?"

"No, no," Scott muttered. He felt weak in his knees. "I just wanted to talk with — you —about your daughter." Scott took a deep breath.

William sat on the end of a log. "Jerry talked with me yesterday by phone," he said in a strange chocked voice. "Is it true?"

"Yes." This would be harder then Scott thought. "I loved your daughter."

William nodded and looked at Scott, a strange look on his face. Scott continued.

"When she died, she was with me in the wreck. I took her body and swam with her to shore."

"Hold on," William interrupted. "You're saying that you were with my daughter when she drowned?" William leaned forward, intent, his eyes on Scott.

"Yes," Scott said. "I swam with her to shore and- "

"You swam with her to shore? I thought she was lost in the wreck."

Scott shook his head, he was miserable. "This is very hard for me." He choked. "Let me tell you what I know, then I'll answer any questions."

"Okay." William leaned back on the log. "Tell me the whole thing." He blinked.

Scott continued. "The accident was so horrible that I blocked it out of my mind and couldn't talk about it. It was like I couldn't remember what happened." Scott paused. He looked up at William. He sat with forced patience, attentive. "I just got out of the hospital, and while I was there," he motioned to his foot, "I remembered what happened."

Scott took another deep breath. "When I swam out of the ocean, and pulled Janet's body to the sand, I saw that she was dead. I was so upset that I couldn't see straight." Scott lowered his head and sniffed.

"And?" William leaned forward.

"No one else was on the island. I took a coconut shell, dug underneath a palm tree, and buried Janet." Scott looked at William, wondering how he would react.

William's voice shook. "This is news." He looked at Scott with sharp interest. "Are you sure?"

"I'll tell you where the palm tree is and Abra can take you there." Scott shuddered. "I just can't go there again, it's too painful."

"I need to call off the search on Quadraline if this is true, Scott." William was looking at Scott. "Why didn't you say something sooner?"

Scott felt himself sinking in fear. " I couldn't remember." He choked.

Janet's dad stood, chest rising and falling, his eyes misty. He shook his head. "I believe what you say. Janet told me about you before she died," William said. "She told me you are very honest. Tell me where the palm tree is, and I'll have Abra take me there."

"It's on a little island. Abra will know which one, because that's where he found me. There's only one lone palm near the end of the sandbar. You can't miss it."

William looked Scott in the eye. "You're sure?"

Scott looked back. He had nothing to hide. "I'm sure."

"I need to go then." William looked a little stunned. "There are people who may still be looking for her body."

The truth was finally known and Scott felt free.

*****

At the apartment, Scott pulled clothes from an old dresser. He tossed them onto a pile behind him, a few pairs of pants, worn out T-shirts, shorts and boxers.

"Jerry, I'm going to give away everything except for maybe one or two sets of clothes. The natives have so little and I want to leave whatever I can."

Jerry picked up a T-shirt. "Won't you need these clothes and things?"

Scott shook his head. "No, they need them more then I do, besides I can get more easily."

Jerry reached down and picked up Scott's yellow Yamaha racing shirt. "Swap this with my Red attitude shirt to remember each other by." He walked to his dresser and pulled out his favorite shirt. "It won't be the same, Scott, We've been through a lot together." He walked to Scott and pushed the shirt into his arm, then gripped him firmly. He reached up quickly and wiped his eye. "Wherever you are, Scott, we're friends for life." Then he laughed a short, sad laugh. "The natives must have got the word out that you're leaving," Jerry looked toward the door. "Here comes some right now."

Scott set the red shirt carefully in his suitcase and walked to the door slowly. He stood watching a group climb the flight of stairs below. They looked up toward him, questioning. As the brown-skinned people gathered around him, they looked at him with eyes full of life. Each one brought something for Scott; pretty shells, woven fans, and other hand-carved items.

A man named Mo gripped Scott's arm firmly. "I will always remember how you helped me," he said with tears in his eyes. "Everyone told me my car was useless, before you came, but now," he gestured with his hand, "it rolls proudly everywhere on this island."

Scott smiled at the memory. He had brought welding rods, and tools with him when he came, things that were very hard to come by in a place like Ebi. One of the first things he had done was help Mo fix his car, and weld its frame back together.

Now Mo gripped his hand wordlessly, leaving a smooth, pretty shell. "For you."

A motherly islander pulled Scott toward her and squeezed him tightly. "I won't be able to fry you bananas anymore, you'll get skinny." She wiped a tear from her eye. "You take care." She handed Scott a hand-woven fan, and then her daughter handed him some fried bananas, wrapped in large green leaves. "So you don't get hungry on the airplane." She smiled.

A boy touched Scott's leg and looked up at him shyly with big round eyes. Scott had been teaching him how to read. "You leave Ebi, Teacher?" he asked sadly. "Who will teach me to read next year?"

Scott looked away and swallowed the lump in his throat. "Jerry and Tony and lots of good teachers will be here to teach you."

The boy looked at Scott with soulful eyes. "You." He handed Scott a small sand dollar and turned to his older sister.

Scott stood sadly, and then remembered that he was packing. "Hold on, everyone." He hurried to the back room and returned with an armload of clothes. "You can have whatever you want." Scott wiped his eyes. "I won't need them where I'm going."

For the next few hours, people dropped by, most brought Scott presents of shells, food and bright bits of coral. Scott's small supply of clothes, and personal items were quickly distributed between the islanders. Later in the evening, one friend brought Scott a woven mat that was a map of the Marshall Islands. On each of the islands a small colorful shell was glued.

"So you can find your way back," he said.

Scott knew it represented hours of skillful work, He folded it carefully and with a sigh, set it in his suitcase with the other shells and gifts. "I will come back some day, I promise I will."

That night, Scott's heart felt heavy as he closed the lid to his suitcase. "Jerry, I came here to teach these people, but the truth is they've taught me." He zipped the cover slowly. " I don't know anyone who can make someone feel as loved as they did for me. I'd give anything to stay here."

Jerry listened in the dignified silence that followed. He was cooking some soup in the kitchen. "Are you hungry?"

Scott shook his head. " No, I don't have an appetite. I think I'll sit on the porch and watch the sunset. I don't know when I'll see it from here again."

A little later, Jerry joined Scott out on the porch. The town was mostly silent in the darkening streets below. A breeze blew the coconut fronds with a rattling noise. The ocean was visible over the roofs of tin and brick. It shone dark against the glowing sunset.

"You know, this is the first time I've really ever sat out here and just watched, Jerry. I can't believe I didn't before now."

"I know." Jerry leaned against the brick wall, "We're always so busy, running here, running there, and we don't realize what's all around us." The two stood silently. "Scott, you know you can reapply to come next year."

"I don't know." Scott shook his head. "I think this is it, Jerry. I don't see how I'll ever come back, and now..." His voice trailed off. The breeze blew a wind chime of island shells with a twinkling sound. "Remember finding those shells out on the reef?"

Jerry turned and lifted the shells with a gentle rattling sound. "That was your first time ever out snorkeling. You were like a kid at Christmas." He chuckled.

"There are no coral reefs in Alaska, so ya." Scott closed his eyes. "It's a whole other world in the ocean here."

The sun slowly disappeared and stars began to replace it in the darkening sky. The two friends sat, experiencing the silent bond only true friends know.

Scott finally stood and walked back into the dark apartment. "See you in the morning, Jerry." He wanted to be alone. Scott lay down. This was his last night.

*****

The morning sun peeked through the open door. Scott sat bolt upright and glanced at the clock. 5:10 AM. Today was the day he was leaving. His spirits sagged with his body as he settled back onto the mattress. He lay awake, moving his foot in small circles. It still hurt, but it wasn't acute like before, just a dim soreness, like a bruise.

Jerry lay snoring peacefully across the room. Scott didn't know how late he had come in. *He must be going through a lot, too,* Scott thought.

Unable to sleep, Scott lay sideways so that he could see the numbers changing on the clock. As in a trance, he saw them change rhythmically; 5:19, 5:20, 5:21. He wished desperately that he could reach out and stop them, but the clock continued its unstoppable march. 5:25. It was ruthless. Time wouldn't stop to let Scott stay in this place he loved so much. He wanted to sleep so he wouldn't have to think about it, but he couldn't. He lay, eyes open. Only seven hours away from a shrinking departure time.

Maybe he should go see people this morning. Scott rolled to the side of the bed again. "Jerry"

"Huh?" Jerry opened his eyes and stopped snoring.

"I'm going to go for a walk down the island. I'll be back."

Jerry nodded and closed his eyes. Scott pulled on some shorts, and painstakingly pulled his tennis shoe onto his hurt foot. Out on the street, the population was not stirring yet, but a pig that had been sleeping near the bottom of the steps ran away from Scott with a shrill yelp. It made Scott jump. Now he was fully awake. He turned toward the gym where the fight had happened. Down the street he wandered, his mind far away. Just a week earlier... he remembered the details: the hot, sweaty run, trying to make Tony leave, and then smacking Tony with the chair leg. He wondered what had happened to Tai. He hadn't seen him since then. Scott turned down the road that led between the coconut plantation and mango trees. The same one he had cut through to save

Tony. He could see the gym with its brick walls, and thatch-covered roof standing ahead, casting a long shadow in the morning sunlight. He walked by slowly, reliving the experience as he glanced through the dusty window. A half-mile further, brick homes stood along the street. Scott wasn't sure whether it was a road or a trail. It was full of potholes and occasionally small trucks, vans and motorcycles rode down the island on it, but mostly people walked or rode bicycles. This early in the morning, there was no traffic.

In one of the houses, a man sat in a chair staring at the path. He saw Scott walking slowly along. A familiar-looking figure emerged from a doorway and hurried toward Scott, It was Tai.

"Scott." He stooped respectfully. "I happened to see you walking by and I wanted to speak with you." He lowered his eyes for a second. "Thank you for keeping me from doing a horrible thing." He clasped Scott's hand and shuddered. " I cannot think when I drink. After I sobered up, I realized what I had almost done, and it scared me so bad I have not been able to drink since then." Scott nodded, a little startled. Tai still held onto his hand. "Scott, I want to tell you something you may not know. Janet's grandmother nursed my mother back to health when I was a small boy." Tai spoke emotionally. "They have stayed friends and she made a deep impression on me. When Janet came to the islands, her grandmother asked my mother and my family to look after her, and when she died, I wanted to kill the man who let her die."

Scott felt himself getting upset. It was hard to hear about Janet. Tai continued as if he didn't notice.

"Also he insulted my sister." Tai scuffed his shoe. "That was the last straw for me, I decided to kill him then. Then you stopped me." He was silent. "Do you know what happened yesterday?" He leaned forward.

Scott looked up. "What?"

"Yesterday Tony sent a letter that apologized to my sister and me." Tai paused and wiped his eye. "I have to forgive him, because that is also what Janet's grandmother taught." Tai pulled out his machete. "Take it. I never want to be reminded of when I almost killed Tony." He shoved it into Scott's hands.

"But this is a valuable tool, how will you open coconuts?" Scott protested.

" I do not want it," Tai said firmly. "I almost killed a man."

*****

Scott walked back down the street in a daze. The island was now waking up around him. Two natives rode by on bikes. Down the road, past the school and through the coconut trees Scott walked. He felt too many emotions to understand. He almost didn't notice where he was walking. Shortly he stood back in front of the apartment.

Jerry was up and stood eating a piece of mango. "Hi, how was your morning walk?" he asked. "Why are you carrying a machete?"

Scott sat down. "Sit down, and I'll tell you all about it..."

*****

The hours of the morning flew by and the hours from noon to two dragged by slowly with their full weight, as if to taunt Scott with their power to make him leave.

He sat with Jerry on the dusty stairs, waiting for Mr. Henrich, too early to leave, too late to do anything else. Scott felt absolutely miserable. Jerry sat wordless. Neither could talk. There was nothing that could be said.

The pickup pulled up five minutes after the hour, and Mr. Henrich waited for Jerry to set Scott's suitcase in the back. The two friends embraced.

"Call me some time. I'll be praying for you." Jerry coughed back his emotions. "I'll miss you, man." As Scott climbed into the truck, he didn't know whether he'd ever see him again. He waved.

The truck drove down the road toward the dock. Scott sat in the passenger side quietly.

"Got your passport, and money, Scott? Everything you need?" Mr. Henrich asked.

Scott nodded. "I'm good."

"Okay." Mr. Henrich pulled up by the dock and popped the truck into neutral. "Your flight doesn't leave until 6:15, if I remember correctly, so you're in no rush. Tell the lady at the Continental desk your name, and she'll give you your ticket."

Mr. Henrich opened his door and hopped out, helping Scott to the ferry's gangplank. He handed him his suitcase. "It's been good having you here." He shook Scott's hand firmly. "I hope you can take the things you learned here and apply them to your life." He gave him a pat. "You've got a lot of life ahead of you, son."

The words felt empty to Scott, like a lame epitaph at a funeral. He looked at Mr. Henrich through misty eyes. "Thanks," he managed.

Scott turned and walked up the ramp to the old ferry. He looked back at Mr. Henrich, watching him get back in his truck and pull away. He waved at the disappearing truck, then let his hand fall to his side. He shuffled to the front carefully and settled down on a wooden seat in the bow.

Whether this boat would be called a ferry anywhere else was anybody's guess. It would depend on what their expectations were. If the fact that it floated, ran, and got from point A to B without capsizing was the definition, then this was a ferry. This particular "ferry" was a war surplus boat that was once a landing craft. Scott watched the natives load fish and coconuts over the side of the boat. He was always amazed at how much these boats could handle.

Scott looked away from the dock to the island. "Goodbye Ebi," he whispered.

The big diesel engine sputtered as it slowly began to churn the water around it. A deckhand untied the big hemp rope and looped it onto the deck. Small waves splashed against the side as the ferry turned toward Quadraline.

Chapter 5

Scott sat, oblivious to the noise around him, which consisted of the chatter of some native women who eyed him curiously, and the loud gnawing of a goat inside a wooden crate. He watched the tip of Ebi disappear past the ferry's right, and then lowered his head.

Just a little bit later, it seemed the boat was arriving at Quadraline. Quadraline was a much different island than the rustic Ebi. A U.S. Air Force base and the Marshall Islands' largest airport rested here, making it the hub of the islands' travel and commerce. Air Force MPs watched as the boat unloaded. Scott stepped onto the dock with the island women and the boat hands, who started unloading the fish crates with an old yellow hand cart. He looked very different from the sharp looking Air Force personnel. His curly red hair puffed above him and his worn clothes didn't match their sharp uniforms.

Relieved not to see anyone familiar, Scott began to walk down the dusty street toward the airport and Air Force barracks. He had been to Quadraline, before so he knew where to go. As he walked, he noticed that his foot began to throb. He shifted his suitcase to the other side. Not much better. To his left, a row of houses stretched along the street. An Air Force engineer named Tom worked with the mission and lived in one of the homes next to the road. He had been helping coordinate the search for Janet. Scott glanced toward his house. He had been there for a get together before, on one of his weekends off. Janet had been there, too. Scott's eyes misted at the memory. They had played Scrabble and eaten popcorn with the other students. A white government truck was now parked in the driveway. He stopped hesitantly. His foot was hurting. He knew they would give him a ride to the airport. Scott stood indecisive. He had worked with Tom's wife, too. She was a small, quiet Indian woman. Scott remembered how she had come to Ebi several times to help in the school. She had been greatly appreciated. She had a soothing motherly presence that calmed the active native children.

Scott took one step, then hesitated. The white shaded porch looked so inviting. But he felt so depressed, he didn't want her to see him cry. He turned back down the road. He didn't want them to remember him like this.

Ten minutes later, and halfway to the airport, Scott began to wish he had stopped and asked for a ride. He was hot and thirsty and his foot caused him to limp.

"I'll stop at the Air Force café and rest," he decided. Only 3:20, and his plane didn't leave until after 6:00. The café/commissary stood next to one of the runways. It was open to anyone who was on the island, many military contractors, and the island's civilians were allowed to shop and eat there.

Scott walked toward the large gray building at the T in the road. The airport was behind the commissary and to its right. As soon as Scott stepped through the door, a refreshing wall of cool air hit him. He half-closed his eyes and let the cool air ruffle through his shirt. It had been a long time since he'd been in an air-conditioned building. He walked to an empty round table and sat down wearily. An officer glanced up at him curiously from another table where he was reading a magazine and sipping a Coke. A plate with a half-eaten burger and chips sat next to him.

Scott realized how thirsty he was, watching the man take a long sip from his refrigerated Coke. He stood and walked to the drink fridge, pulled a cold orange soda from the back rack and walked to the counter.

"That will be a quarter."

Scott reached in his pocket, fumbled around, and handed her a quarter. "Thank you." He walked back to his chair and sat, slowly drinking his soda and glancing around the store. Just like a grocery store with a military-like touch, no frills. On his side was a small deli and an area with black tables and chairs. The deli served sandwiches, hotdogs, and muffins, it looked like. Not much else.

After his drink, Scott walked back out into the hot street, feeling more refreshed. He hadn't been hungry at all though, not normal for him.

"I must be too upset to be hungry," he thought. The five minutes it took Scott to walk to the small civilian terminal passed slowly. The island's palm trees swayed in the humid wind, and a sun shown down from a clear blue sky.

The civilian airport was a small brown building. A couple of parked taxis were in the small passenger pickup area. A dark-skinned man with a blue taxi hat relaxed in the shade of the building, smoking a cigarette.

He nodded politely to Scott as he limped up to the door. Scott pushed the glass door open and stepped into the seemingly dark airport office — the bright outside light made it seem dark. A single counter with a crooked Continental sign hanging above it stood by the luggage area. Another empty desk had **Charter flights meet here**, printed in bold letters above it. To the side, a door led out to the tarmac.

A woman with a Continental nametag sat on a stool behind the desk, reading a novel. She folded the page over and looked up at Scott. "Can I help you?"

"Yes." Scott leaned against the counter. "I have a ticket on the 6:15 Continental flight to Guam." Scott rummaged for his driver's license. "I was told to get my ticket here."

The lady took Scott's ID, glanced at it briefly, and ran her finger down a list of names, "Hmmm, let's see. Yes, you are on that flight." She closed her ledger book. "Let me get you your ticket." She disappeared through a door into a back office and left Scott standing by the desk.

She returned and handed Scott his ticket, "Just carry your bag out to the plane when it boards, and make sure to be here by 6:00. It's 4:00 right now." She smiled.

"Thanks, and do you have a pay phone?" Scott gripped his bag and looked hesitantly around the lobby.

"Yes, it's outside and around the corner." She pointed out the door.

Scott walked out the door again, carrying his suitcase and ticket under his arm. The taxi man tipped his hat to him as he walked past him toward the weathered phone booth. The smell of cigarette smoke drifted to Scott as he set his suitcase down and lifted the receiver. He took a deep breath, then hung the phone up again. He rummaged in his suitcase until he pulled out a small coin purse. He counted out dimes and nickels until he had a small handful, then set them by the phone. **Calls to U.S. 10 cents a minute** was written in black marker on a piece of paper taped across the top. He picked the phone up, took another deep breath, then punched in the familiar number. He waited, then dropped four dimes into the slot.

On the other end, he could hear it ringing. It rang three times, then Scott heard the phone being lifted from the hook. "Hello this is Robert, and with whom am I speaking?"

"Hi, Dad." Scott gulped.

"Son, you better not be calling collect, I don't have a money tree here."

Scott tried not to sound hurt. "Dad, I'm paying for this call. I uh—"

"I'm glad to see you're responsible enough to pay for your own long distance calls." The voice was sarcastic.

Scott bit his lip. "Dad, just let me talk to Mom."

"Hold on."

Scott heard his Dad yelling faintly in the background, then a few seconds later he heard his mom's voice.

"Hi, honey, how are you?" His mom sounded tired but glad to talk with him.

"Honestly, Mom, not that good." Scott twisted the phone wire and tried to sit on his suitcase.

"Why, honey? What's happened? I haven't talked with you since April, that was the last time you called." Her voice held a bit of hurt indignation.

"I know, Mom." Scott fidgeted, "I haven't been to Quadraline for a couple of months now." How was he supposed to tell his mom that he didn't like calling home? All the bad news only depressed him and made him angry, and his mom always complained to him about Dad. He felt like an emotional sewer drain every time he talked to her. His uncle Matthew had died five years ago when he was sixteen, but the family had never quite healed from its repercussions.

"What's the problem?" Her voice bounced through his mind.

"Uh." Scott gulped. He did not want to break down now. "I know this is abrupt, Mom, but I'm coming home. I got really sick from an infection so I'm flying to Guam where Uncle John is, then home to the States after I'm well."

"Oh my!" she gasped. Her voice became angry again. "Why didn't they call and tell us?"

Scott twisted the phone around his ear uncomfortably. "It's probably because I forgot to put you on my emergency contact numbers list and they only had Uncle John's."

"Well, at least Uncle John could have called us!" Her voice sounded indignant.

"Mom, Mom," Scott pleaded. "Please don't get upset, I'll be fine. I haven't even talked to Uncle John myself, only our mission director did. Mr. Henrich just told me he's expecting me and he'll be waiting at the airport when I land."

"I know why he didn't call to tell us. He hasn't spoken to us since Matthew's funeral. He was very upset with Robert over what he said to him there." Her voice came in a resolute tone, like she had just discovered something important.

"What was that?" Scott cradled the phone and dropped another dime in.

"Your dad told John that his brother, your Uncle Matthew, had been screwing you up with his out-dated biblical psychology, and that it was probably for the best that he had fallen and died. Of course, he said that before John was an Air Force Chaplain, and when he'd drunken one too many."

"Dad said that?" Scott's hand shook slightly. A tear suddenly tried to force itself from the corner of his eye. He wiped it away angrily.

"Oh, honey don't be upset." Her voice became soothing. "I just thought you should know what had happened so you don't go in blind, you know as smart as a dove, as harmless as a snake, like your Uncle Matthew said."

"Mom! You said it backwards. You don't even know what it means!" Scott felt himself getting angry despite his weakened condition.

"Don't be upset, dear. I didn't mean to turn it around. Sometimes I'm dyslexic. But tell me what happened, I'm very concerned."

Scott told his mom how he had cut his foot and the whole incident from beginning to end. "That's all I know, Mom, it's so bizarre," he finished.

His mom's voice came over the line "Scott, it's so strange that you're leaving so suddenly. I think something else has to be going on. Either that, or God really wants you to leave for some reason."

Scott's face tightened. "If God wanted me to leave, then I could just tell Him to go to hell!" Scott was surprised at the intensity of his words. "I love it here, Mom." He stopped talking so that his voice could steady.

"Oh, don't talk like that." She sounded worried. "Do you need money, dear?"

"No, Mom," Scott felt good to say that. "I've been saving the money I've earned these last six months, and I have enough."

"Well, that's a good thing then, because I wasn't looking forward to asking Robert to wire you money. It seems money is becoming a real issue here lately."

"Uh, huh," Scott said. He was thinking about his dad's remark about money when he first called.

"You know Matthew's old construction company?"

"Yeah?" Scott was paying attention again.

"Your dad just loaned his old foreman, Owen, $200,000 to help pay for some big mistakes he's made running it, and your dad's practice has not been bringing in as much as normal."

"Why did he loan that —" Scott searched for words, "guy money in the first place?" he demanded.

"Well you know how your Dad and Owen have always been real good buddies since high school." She lowered her voice. "That's how—"

"Mom, hold on." Scott dropped a couple more coins into the slot. "I was low on minutes. Okay, continue."

"Well, that's how Owen got a job as Matthew's foreman in the first place, because your dad recommended him. So when Matthew died and Owen took the company over, and of course married Matthew's wife and everything, your dad wanted to help him out since he's family now."

"He's not family," Scott declared. "He married Aunt Tiffany way too soon after Matthews death, only two weeks, and I'm almost sure they were living together before that." Scott paused. "So you're saying that Owen has bankrupted Matthew's business — which he stole — I mean didn't deserve, and now Dad's bailing him out?"

"He didn't steal it, honey, it was his to take."

"Whatever," Scott muttered.

"Oh things aren't the best around here," she continued. "Aunt Tiff and Owen aren't doing that well, either. I think they're going through some marital stress. Aunt Tiff misses Matthew, is what I think it is." She sighed. "It's strange how she never got along with Matthew when they were married, but now she wishes she could go back." Scott heard her breathing in the phone. "But your father knows how to help them, so I'm sure everything will be alright."

"Just because Dad is a psychiatrist, doesn't mean he knows everything," Scott snapped. "He can't put broken things back together." He stopped. "I'm sorry, Mom, I just haven't wanted to hear about this. That's just one of the many reasons I love it out here."

"Oh, Scott, everything will work out for the best, I'm sure." Mom's voice was soothing.

Scott heard someone shouting in the background. "Jean, are you still on the phone? I need your help."

"Say goodbye to your dad, Scott." Scott heard her hand the phone away. "Here, Robert, it's Scott, say bye."

"Hi, Scott." His dad's voice came over the phone. "So you're sick, your mother says?"

Scott shifted legs. "Yes, but I'm getting better now, I'm sure Mom will tell you all about it."

"Okay then. Well, take care of yourself."

"Okay Dad, I'll talk to you later."

"All right, son. Bye." The line went silent, and a dime rolled out of the change dish.

Scott felt relieved that he was going to Guam instead of straight home for some reason...

He hung up the phone. He closed his eyes and shook his head emphatically from side to side, as if to forget about the chaos he had just heard. He didn't want to go back to that world. There were too many painful memories there. Scott felt a little bit between a rock and a hard place. Here in the islands, he had the pain of Janet's death, and he had to leave now anyways. And he had just heard a sample of what he had at home. Maybe he needed to just go to a new place and start a new life. He was single and twenty-one.

Scott had a phone number scribbled in pencil on a small stub of paper. It was smudged and dirty from being in his pocket. Scott put his extra dime back in the phone. He paused. He hadn't talked to his Uncle Matthew's brother since the funeral, either. He wasn't sure what to say, as he had only met him once.

Well, no time to worry about that now. Scott dialed the number and listened as the phone rang. Five times it rang, then a message machine answered. "Hello, you've reached the office of Chaplain John. I'm away from my office at the moment, but leave your name and phone number after the tone and I will return your call."

Scott waited for the beep. "Hi, John, this is Scott," he almost mumbled. "I'm coming in on Continental 63 at nine tonight. I'm looking forward to seeing you then." Scott paused for a second, but his mind was blank, so he hung up the phone.

Scott felt the wind blowing gently against him. The air felt muggy. He looked up behind him and saw a large, dark billowing wall of clouds filling half the sky.

"That's where the breeze is coming from," he muttered. Even as Scott stood there watching, the clouds moved, rolling in gigantic billows, filling the clear blue sky.

He grabbed his suitcase and hurried around the side of the building into the airport office.

"Looks like a storm is coming."

A gust of wind blew through the door as Scott entered. The lady looked up startled from her book. "Oh." She stepped off her stool and looked out. "Why yes, it looks like it will rain."

"That won't delay anything will it?" Scott raised an eyebrow apprehensively.

The lady glanced at some charts she had. "We'll see, but it shouldn't. A lot of Air Force personnel are flying out on this flight, so I don't think it will be canceled."

"Summer vacation, is that where you're going?"

Scott shook his head. "No, I'm flying to Guam to visit a relative." He didn't want to explain further.

"Oh, that's nice. Guam's a fun place to visit. If you get a chance, there's some great diving there."

"Okay." Scott nodded. He didn't want to talk about it. Walking to the window, he looked out on the tarmac. A few raindrops had been blown against the window, though the clouds hadn't reached them yet.

He sat down in one of the uncomfortable chairs, and watched as the clouds rolled forward in a misty advance, followed by a wall of water. The rain came in sheets down the runway, until the first gust hit the small airport with a loud watery hammering sound. Water ran down the window and around the ditches outside. Scott could hear lighting cracking and thunder rumbling outside.

Several vans pulled up outside, and some Air Force men came into the little airport. Some were laughing and joking with each other. Scott just sat by the window, watching the falling rain, shoulders slouched.

The chairs filled up around Scott. The Air Force men sat talking together, and a few men smoked outside under the canopy. A few minutes later, the airplane appeared from behind a mist of cloud and water, steeply cutting downwards, its landing lights blinking. It was a Boeing 737. The jet descended out of the clouds and bounced a couple of times at the end of the runway. It taxied to a stop just outside on the tarmac.

"Please be patient." The Continental lady had switched into work mode. "We need to unload the passengers first, and take some luggage off before we can board. It will probably be about half an hour." She was now helping a line of passengers get tickets, busily moving about.

A ramp opened from the side of the airplane and Scott watched as people began to come out. Some had umbrellas, and those who didn't shared or hurried quickly to the terminal's cover. Most looked to be military, but one stuck out vividly. A dark-haired woman wearing an attractive sweater stepped from the airplane. She started to hurry along the tarmac, but a man offered her his umbrella and they walked quickly into the airport, then separated. She walked over to an empty chair and plopped down, glancing around the lobby, catching Scott's eye. Military men of all shapes and sizes stood waiting to board the plane, while others loaded into vans and taxis waiting outside. The lady must have been waiting to re-board, just like several others, Scott figured. He knew the planes hopped from island to island on their way to Guam, dropping off and picking up assorted tourists and military people.

In her seat, the woman was thinking. She sighed and glanced at the name. **Quadraline Civil Airport.** She shuffled through her ticket book. This was the last stop before Guam. Thank God!

Looking around the airport, she saw the familiar light blue uniforms, then curiously she saw a man sitting by the window. He had a red afro, and was wearing worn looking shorts and a white T-shirt. He obviously wasn't from the Air Force.

I wonder if he's a bum? she thought. She watched him a little longer, then looked away, not wanting to be caught staring.

"And now all our passengers who were already on Flight 63 to Guam may re-board," the Continental woman announced through a raspy loudspeaker. She stood by the gate, glancing at tickets while the passengers filed back outside and hurried back to the plane, holding umbrellas in an attempt to stay dry. A man at the door collected the umbrellas and returned them back so more groups could make the dash.

The lady with the dark hair stood and joined the rapidly shortening line. She couldn't help but look curiously at the man with the red hair again. He had a sad look on his face, and his blue eyes seemed a little red. She felt a tinge of sympathy. He looked up and their eyes met briefly. She glanced away embarrassed, feeling her face flush.

"Can I see your ticket, Ma'am?" the stewardess asked her.

"Oh yes, I'm sorry," she said, flustered. She handed the stewardess her ticket. "Have a pleasant flight." The stewardess smiled and watched her hurry out to the airplane.

Soon the general boarding began. There were only about 20 people getting on now. Scott lingered despite the empting line. He knew that once he walked up the ramp to the airplane, this world would close behind him, and he wanted to stay here for as long as possible.

He looked out the window. The weather seemed to match his feelings perfectly. Thunder in the distance, and wind blowing the rain sideways across the runway.

"Final call for Flight 63 to Guam. That would be you, sir." The lady looked at Scott from behind her counter. Scott stood, gripped his suitcase and walked to the counter. He handed his ticket over, had it clipped, then walked out into the rain. A soaking attendant handed Scott an umbrella and helped him hurry to the airplane.

"May I stow your bag, sir?"

Scott let go of his bag and stepped inside the airplane.

He stood looking down a crowded aisle. The engines were warming up, and a flight attendant was latching the door behind him. Scott looked at his ticket. 32A. All the way to the back of the plane. He had to step sideways down the aisle. He felt very uncomfortable wading through the gauntlet of soldiers.

Scott moved to the back of the plane. 32B. There was the dark-haired lady.

"Excuse me, that's my seat." Scott motioned at his ticket.

Oh, that quaint fellow, she thought. She leaned back to avoid him brushing her as he squeezed past.

Scott sat down, leaned his head against the small oval window, and gazed into the rain. The tires had barely left the tarmac before they were over the ocean. He hardly noticed as rain and wind buffeted the wings. Clouds soon blotted out the ocean below as the airplane climbed. Scott felt dejected. He was wrapped up in his own world, oblivious to the woman next to him.

It seemed like only a minute had passed before Scott heard a voice. "Excuse me, would you like something to drink?"

Scott turned. He looked up at the stewardess. Scott began to decline, then he changed his mind. "I'll take a glass of water." He gripped the outstretched cup. "Thanks." Scott turned back toward the window.

"So what are you doing out on these islands? I notice you're not military like everyone else." A female voice caused Scott to turn back.

He stared for a second. "No, I'm not military." He stopped talking, then realized she was waiting for him to say more. "I'm a teacher at a mission school. Well, I was a teacher." Scott looked away miserably.

"Why are you going to Guam?" This lady was persistent.

"I'm going because of an unfortunate series of events. I won't bore you with them, though." Scott looked back toward the window.

"Oh no, I'm interested." The lady leaned forward. "My name's Laura, what's yours?"

"Scott."

"So what is this long series of unfortunate events?" Her eyes sparkled ever so slightly.

This lady won't quit, Scott thought. He glanced at her apprehensively, trying to decide how much to say. She waited, arms resting on her lap. "I was a teacher in the Marshall Islands at a mission school." A shadow crossed his face "I cut my foot shark fishing. It got infected..." He told her a brief overview of how he had almost died. "So now I'm on my way home," he finished.

She leaned forward, visibly trying to figure him out. Scott looked away.

"If you don't mind me asking, is that the reason you're so sad?"

"I seem sad?" he asked, as if it wasn't obvious.

"Yes, you don't hide it well." She shrugged.

"There is one thing." Scott hesitated. "I don't know."

Laura drew back in her seat. "You don't have to tell me."

"No it's okay," Scott said. "There was a girl." He cleared his throat. "Her name was Janet. She died when our mission sailboat sank."

"I'm so sorry," Laura said. "I didn't mean to pry."

Scott settled in the seat. "It's all right."

"Excuse me, would you two like something more to drink?" The stewardess was back.

Laura and Scott looked up together. "No thanks," they responded in unison.

The airplane was full of sleeping men now, and it was dark except for the soft glimmer of the moon reflecting on the plane's wings. Scott looked out the small window.

Laura interrupted the silence. "Janet was very special to you wasn't she?"

Scott nodded. "That's why they made me leave, because things just fell apart after she died." He didn't tell her about Tony or hitting him with the chair. He didn't know how well he could explain that.

"I understand how you feel." Laura sighed. "You know, when your life feels like it's just absolutely falling apart." She seemed comfortable talking with him now. "Four years ago, I was divorced, and it was a rough road. I didn't know things could get that bad. I drank a lot." She paused, searching Scott's face for interest. "Just six months ago, I found the Lord, and things have been going uphill since then." She chatted on, telling him about her life, and how she had quit drinking.

Scott watched her quietly. For some reason listening to her helped him get out of his shell. "So why are you flying to Guam?" he asked.

"To visit my brother in the Air Force. I felt like I needed to get away from Idaho." She continued, telling him about her nursing job. The plane was slanting downwards.

"All passengers, please remain seated, we are on our final approach."

Laura looked up startled. "That was sure quick."

People started stirring as the plane descended to the glittering lights below.

Chapter 6

The Boeing 737 came in over the water. Scott saw a blur of ground separate from the dark ocean. The tires bounced once on the runway before the plane settled down, all engines screaming and flaps up. He nervously gripped his seat as the plane began to decelerate.

"It's amazing how fast that was. We were over the water, and boom! Seconds later on the runway. We didn't even see the ground until we were on it." Laura nodded and leaned her head back. "I'm glad we're here. This trip seemed like forever."

A shiny head a couple of seats ahead of them turned and waved a large tattooed arm. "We'll be on the ground shortly, folks," he mimicked the flight attendant. "I always wonder in what form I'll be on the ground?"

The guys behind him laughed and thumped him on the back. "Sit down Frank, we're already on the ground."

"Joke wouldn't have been funny earlier." Frank turned in his seat.

As the plane taxied to the gate, Scott began to feel light-headed. It was like his mind was still on Ebi but his body had moved, as if the whole flight was a dream, and he was now waking from it.

Laura was talking to him. "It was nice to meet you. I don't meet mission teachers all the time."

Scott felt his pulse race. "Uh, ya it was nice." He didn't look at her.

She cleared her throat, "I'll bump into you around maybe? How long will you be in Guam?"

Scott's mind didn't register that she was hinting, his mind was too wrapped in the pain of Janet and leaving, and this re-adjustment his mind rebelled against. "Just long enough to get back to the States," he said without emotion.

Laura looked disappointed. "You'll be here for a while, though. We might be in the same area?" She didn't want to be any more obvious.

Scott didn't say anything, so neither did she. He was too absorbed in thought. She bit her lip and turned, frustrated.

"Your customs declaration form." The flight attendant pushed a slip at Laura and Scott.

Scott ignored the pilot's welcome speech. He stood and shuffled into the aisle, following Laura as she exited the airplane.

"Thanks for flying with us." Scott hardly nodded as he passed the friendly pilot. On the jet way, they joined a stream of people walking toward the terminal.

At the top of a flight of stairs, they entered the domed airport. People were waiting, kissing and hugging around them.

"There's my brother," Laura squealed, and then frowned. *Who's he talking to?* she thought. *He's not looking for me.* He was talking to a man holding a sign. "That isn't someone you know holding the 'Scott' sign, is it?" She turned finding Scott in the crowd.

"That is." Scott stared. He recognized John instantly. He hadn't changed at all in five years. John looked just like he did at the funeral, but definitely happier. He was standing talking animatedly with another man, his sign hanging limply from one hand, while he gestured with the other.

"He's talking to my brother." Laura pointed. "That's my brother."

The two walked forward until they were close enough to reach out and touch the two men.

"Charlie" Laura made a waving motion. "I'm here." Both John and Charlie looked up at the same time, ending their conversation.

"Hi, sis." Charlie jumped forward and caught Laura in a bear hug. She giggled.

John reached out and shook Scott's hand. "Glad you made it. How's your foot?" He looked down at Scott's shoe. "Which one is it?"

"Oh," Scott said, embarrassed. "It's my right foot. It's doing a lot better now."

"Well, from the way your director talked, I considered bringing an ambulance." John stepped back and surveyed Scott. "Maybe that was overkill."

"Oh, no, I'll be fine." Scott grinned, embarrassed.

"That's good. Let me introduce you to a friend of mine from the base." John turned to the man standing by Laura. "This is Charles."

Scott stepped forward and shook his hand. "Nice meeting you."

"This is my little sister, Laura," Charles said.

The group chatted for a minute before John waved goodbye and beckoned Scott. "Let's get your bag. The baggage claim is this way. We still have to go through customs, so let's try to get home before your aunt Ruth is in bed." John started walking, then had to turn and wait for Scott. "Sorry, I forgot."

Scott limped behind him. "It's alright." He forced a smile, despite how tired he felt.

Laura stood talking with her brother. She glanced at Scott for a long second as he and John disappeared into the crowd. "You know his uncle?"

"Oh yeah, he's a friend of mine from the base, great guy," Charles said.

"Oh."

Charles started to walk away. "We just happened to be waiting for you two at the same time, worked out well."

"We just happened to be sitting next to each other on the plane, too." Laura was contemplating something. She shook her head.

"You think he's an interesting guy?" Charles said, suddenly a teasing sparkle in his eye.

"Stop, Charles," she sighed. "I had enough of that from you in high school."

"Gosh, don't be so defensive." Charles raised his hands in mock innocence.

Laura shook her head. "He's all depressed about his girlfriend's death. Anyway, it's not like he's even interested in other girls." She laughed. "What an interesting thought."

*****

John swung Scott's suitcase into the back of the Toyota Corolla. He closed the hatch and walked around the car. He fumbled with the keys in the dark for a second, then got in.

"So what does it feel like to be on Guam?" John asked. He switched on the headlights as he pulled out of the parking lot.

"Good, well fine, I guess." Scott sat stiffly in the seat next to John.

John didn't say anything for a minute as he steered into traffic. The car glided through the dark streets away from the lights of the airport.

"We'll be to Anderson soon."

"What's it like to be a chaplain there?"

"Oh, it's a lot of fun and work. These men all need God just like everyone else. There are a lot of thirsty souls in uniform." He cleared his throat and reached down between the seat with one hand. "I have something I want you to have."

He held up a green book, held shut by a big rubber band. He handed it to Scott.

Scott held it up and stared at it in the dim light from the dash. "What is it?" He looked at John curiously.

"It's a journal of Matthew's." He flicked the turn signal on and turned onto another road. "When I was packaging up all the stuff Tiffany didn't want when Matthew died, I decided to keep it. Matthew talks about you in it, so I thought you'd want it."

"Oh." Scott pulled on the rubber band that wrapped the journal. "Thanks." He didn't want to think about his uncle right now. It depressed him.

They drove up to the gates of Anderson. The guard waved John through with a quick glance at his pass.

The base was more orderly then the rest of the island, Scott noticed. Even in the dark he could see several large buildings in neat rows.

"We're almost there." John motioned. Scott looked up at a complex of houses they approached. The Corolla pulled up to one and John switched off the engine. "You're welcome to stay here as long as you need to."

Scott stepped out of the car and looked up at the darkened building. A light shone from behind a curtain. Under the porch light, Scott could see tan paint and a brass nameplate on the door. Chaplain John and Ruth Olsen.

"Ruth must be up waiting." The front door opened before he reached the first step.

"Hello, Scott, so good to see you." Ruth laughed and stepped down the stairs. She squeezed Scott in a warm hug. "I'm glad you're here, you're going be okay now." She held him out at arm's length. "Oh my, you've grown up so much."

Inside Ruth bustled around getting John and Scott a glass of cold water. She paused briefly to kiss John. "Let me show you your room Scott." She beckoned. "It's late and I'm sure you're exhausted after your long flight. We'll all be able to talk more tomorrow."

Scott was grateful to be able to close the guest room door and be alone. Letting his suitcase fall to the floor, he sank onto the bed. The soft down comforter squished under him. A reading lamp was next to the bed where he sat.

Scott sighed and lay back, staring up at the pretty curtains above him. A breeze ruffled them. He picked up the green book John had given him and turned it over in his hand. It was old and faded. On the front was stamped **Journal.**

My uncle's journal, he mused. *I wonder why John gave me this?* He settled back onto the soft pillow and let his heavy eyelids close slowly. His hand relaxed and the book slipped onto the bed. He was asleep.

Ruth checked on him and quietly switched the lights off. Continuing down the hall and into her bedroom, Ruth changed clothes and climbed into bed next to her husband. She rolled over with a sigh. "I just don't know what to think dear." She snuggled up to John in the darkness. "I think he's lonely, John, and needs someone to talk to, is what I think."

John grunted. "I wonder if he'll open up with us."

Ruth laid her head on the pillow. "What he needs is a special friend, a girl he can trust, you know."

"Well, I don't fit that ticket," John said. "At least the girl part."

"If Scott's smart, he'll realize that he can trust you with anything."

John cleared his throat. "Speaking of girls, Scott flew here with Charles's sister. I guess they sat next to each other on the plane. Laura, I think her name is. She's really pretty, but Scott seemed indifferent to her. I don't think he's interested." He gave a short laugh, then became serious. "I gave him Matthew's journal you know."

"Already?" Ruth asked, surprised.

"Well, I know he'll read it, so I figured there was no sense in waiting. He won't be here forever." John sighed.

The two lay in the darkness for a second, then Ruth cleared her throat. "Charles has a sister visiting? If she's anything like Charles, she might be really good for Scott to visit with."

John grunted. "Not a bad idea, she'd be good company for him, if he was interested."

Ruth chuckled. "Well, I'll see what I can do about that, dear."

The house was silent now. Only the hum of night insects was heard as the dark night nestled on it's sleeping inhabitants.

*****

Scott woke, opening his eyes to the sight of pretty wallpaper. Sleeping on a soft feather bed was unusual. He stretched his back slightly. It felt almost like he'd slept on it wrong. Slipping out of bed, he walked to the door. He could smell pancakes frying from the kitchen.

"Good morning, Scott," Ruth said cheerfully. "I hope you're hungry."

Scott sat on a stool while Ruth poured him a glass of guava juice. He rubbed his eyes sleepily.

"John had to run to the office earlier this morning, and I'm going in to my clerical job in half an hour," Ruth continued. "You have an appointment to visit Doctor Lewis at 11. I've arranged for someone to come by and give you a ride." She pushed a plate of banana pancakes in front of Scott.

"Who's picking me up and when?" Scott held his knife in mid air over his plate.

"Oh, you know Charlie's sister, Laura? I called Charles this morning and asked if Laura would take you, she'll be here around 10:45." She was facing the fridge, so Scott couldn't see her expression, but her voice was suspiciously light.

"I see." Scott bit into his pancake. He thought he saw the hint of a smirk on the corner of her mouth when she turned around again.

"Looks like you better get changed and comb that hair of yours, because its already 10:15" Ruth loaded dishes into the dish washer.

Scott took another bite of his pancake and chewed thoughtfully. "I'll be ready." He didn't want to appear concerned.

*****

Scott sat in the living room. The house was silent. His aunt had just left and now he was waiting. Scott thought about how Ruth had given him a slight lift of her eyebrows and said to "Have fun."

He absently flipped open the cover to his uncle's green journal. He recognized Matthew's distinctive scrawl immediately.

Dear God, Today was a day just like yesterday. I worked on the project on Happy Lane, same old backbreaking labor. I get so tired, sometimes I wonder why I ever chose this profession. It will make me an old man before I want to admit it—but on to more happy subjects, I went out with Timothy today for lunch. We were talking about trust, and some biblical examples he was showing me. What are you trying to teach me? Apparently he's been preaching a series on trust at his church, and he's been learning a lot of new things. I'll tell you all about—

Scott was cut short by a distinctive knock on the door. He closed the journal, tucked it under his arm, and walked to the door. He could see a woman standing through the glass.

"Hi." Scott swung the door open. "I'm just getting my shoes on."

Laura stood fidgeting, "So, the main hospital, right?"

Scott was aware that Laura obviously felt uncomfortable. "Yes, I need to see a Doctor Lewis." He glanced up from tying his shoe. "I'm sorry you have to take me, I hope this isn't an inconvenience for you." *Oops, that came out wrong,* he thought desperately.

"Oh no, don't be sorry, it isn't." Laura blushed. "I didn't have anything planned for this morning, so it worked out well."

*****

Laura had awakened to eat breakfast with her brother, Charles and her sister-in-law, Mabel. They were chatting pleasantly and catching up on events when the phone had rung.

Charles had cradled the phone on his shoulder, listening to the person talking on the other end. "Mmm." He looked up at Laura. "Mhmm, mhmm. Let me ask her and I'll get right back to you." He hung up the phone and turned toward the table where Laura and Mabel sat. "John just called, and he was wondering if you would be willing to take Scott, the guy you met on the airplane, to the doctor this morning."

"This morning?" Laura gasped and nearly dropped the muffin she was eating. "I, uh, how would, and why would I take him?"

"Oh, you can use my old truck. John's wife had him call because she thought you might do Scott some good." Charles's eyes were twinkling teasingly again. "Maybe my instincts at the airport were right."

"Do him good?" Laura crossed her arms and sat back. "Right."

"He didn't even seem interested in talking to me before." Her mind was racing. Had Scott asked for her to take him? Maybe he was too shy to just talk to her himself.

Charles and her sister-in-law were talking. "So do you want to?" He turned to Laura, holding the phone in his hand. "I told him I'd call him right back."

"Uh sure, I guess I can." She slumped. Might as well.

*****

Laura stood at the address her brother had given her, his handwritten map in her hand. Scott looked nervous to her.

In the truck, they buckled in and turned to each other. Laura spoke first. "So you didn't ask for me to come pick you up?" Scott shook his head. "Oh." Laura lifted her chin and looked away.

"I don't mind, though," Scott stammered. "I think it was my Aunt Ruth's idea."

"Oh, okay, but don't feel like I'm trying to spend time with you if you don't want to be around me."

"No no," Scott protested. "If I've seemed unfriendly, it's only because I've been really under the weather with everything that's been happening. I felt like I was overwhelming you with how I've been feeling."

Laura felt satisfied. "Okay, but only if you want me to take you." She started the engine. Scott leaned back in his seat and sighed. "And don't worry about overwhelming me with your emotions. I think I can handle them." Laura looked at Scott sideways with a short laugh.

"Okay, good to hear that." Scott relaxed. "How far is the hospital?"

"I have a map. Here, help me." Laura handed Scott the directions. "Tell me when to turn."

"I'm embarrassed about all this fuss with my foot."

"Doesn't quite fit your style?" Laura cocked her head. "Not macho hero enough?"

Scott laughed. "Something like that."

Just a few minutes later, they pulled up at the hospital, an Air Force building with palm trees planted along its tan side. Inside, the receptionist asked Scott for his Air Force service card.

"Oh, actually, I'm not in the Air Force," he explained. "Chaplain John, my uncle, made me an appointment with Doctor Lewis this morning." Scott pushed the slip of paper Ruth had given him toward the lady.

She read it. "Oh, okay. He'll be with you in one minute. You and your wife can wait in the lobby." She motioned.

"Oh, actually it's friend," Laura corrected.

"Ya, that." Scott said.

The lady laughed. "Could have fooled me." she said cheerily.

Scott forced a laugh. He and Laura sat down in the small lobby and looked at each other uncomfortably, then laughed. He shrugged.

"Scott?" A balding military doctor in a white coat and white mustache stood looking into the lobby.

"Here." Scott raised his hand and stood.

"Right this way, soldier." The doctor motioned.

Scott followed him into a examining room.

"Let me see your wound there." The grandfatherly doctor helped Scott sit on a paper-covered examining table. He watched as Scott removed his shoe and sock. "Ouch, you get the purple heart for that one, ace." He pulled on a pair of white gloves.

"Oh, actually, I'm not a soldier. I'm a student missionary." Scott raised his foot for the doctor to see.

"Hmm... I don't see your types here everyday." The doctor stood back and stared at Scott. "And where were you a student missionary?"

"Ebi, Marshall Islands." Scott then explained what had happened.

"Hmmm." The doctor scratched his chin. He had been examining the wound. "It looks like its healing well. Just keep it clean and I'll prescribe you some ointment for it. Can't do much else for you."

Scott shook his head. It was so stupid that Mr. Henrich had made him leave, he thought bitterly. "Doctor?" he asked.

"Yes, son?"

"Is it all right if I swim in the ocean?"

"Well, I don't know about that." Doctor Lewis leaned against the counter with a twinkle in his eye. "Why? Are you wanting to go looking for mermaids?"

"I'm interested in checking out some of the reefs around here." Scott looked expectant.

"Well, I'd say that if you give it a couple of days, and it's healing nicely, I think you could. But don't you go re opening it," he warned. "It will be easy to cut and I don't want you out there bleeding. The sharks here in Guam aren't very forgiving.

"Thanks, doctor." Scott put his sock and shoe back on.

Doctor Lewis opened the cupboard and handed Scott a small bottle of ointment. "Apply this once a day, and you'll be fine." He smiled.

Laura was waiting in the lobby. "Must not be too bad," she said. "You look happier."

Scott smiled. "Didn't even need to come to the doctor."

The receptionist waved Scott off at the counter, telling him that his uncle had taken care of everything. Out in the parking lot, they both climbed into the muggy truck.

"Oh, I sure didn't park in the shade." Laura fanned herself.

Scott vigorously rolled down the window. "I'm glad that's over, anyways." He tapped his foot against the floorboard.

"So now what?" Laura asked.

Scott wanted to make sure Laura knew he wasn't just using her for the ride. "Why don't we go get some lunch or something and visit a little? I don't have anything on my agenda if you don't," he said. "I'm buying."

"Well I suppose that if you're not busy, I can make room in my busy vacation schedule for lemonade," Laura quipped. She was smiling, actually blushing a little bit. She liked how the tables had turned a little. "So how are you finding Guam?" she asked as she turned onto a street heading for the airbase gate.

"It's good. I've only been here less then 20 hours now, and I've talked with you more then anybody else."

"Uh huh." Laura nodded. "From what my brother says, your uncle John is a great guy."

"Well, he's my uncle indirectly," Scott explained. "His dead brother, Matthew, is my real uncle because he was married to my dad's sister. I just call him Uncle John. Makes things simpler."

"I see."

"The one thing Uncle John has done since I got here was kind of strange, though." Scott held up the green diary with **Journal** stamped on it.

"What?" Laura asked, confused.

"Last night on the way from the airport, he gave me this." Scott held the book up with a little shake. "He said it was a journal of my Uncle Matthew's, and there were some things in it I should read. Kinda weird right?"

Laura looked curiously at the book Scott was holding. "Well, you should read it. There has to be a reason."

"He said Matthew talked about me in it." He began to undo the rubber band. "I just started looking at it this morning before you arrived."

"Well, why don't we both look at it together here in Dina's diner, over a glass of lemonade?" Laura pulled into the parking lot. "That is, if you don't mind me," she added.

"No, I wouldn't mind. I'd actually like that, I think," Scott responded. "Let's do it."

Inside the diner, the two sat in a window booth and a waiter took their order: two burgers with fries and drinks.

Laura was sitting across the booth from Scott. He handed her the green journal. "Take a look," he said. "I'm kinda like 'Oh well, I don't care,' concerning my family's dark secrets, so don't feel like you're intruding." There was a hint of bitterness in his voice.

"Okay, so long as I'm not intruding." Laura unfastened the rubber band. "It's not like I haven't had my own life's drama. I'm not a judgmental person. I couldn't be without going crazy."

Scott nodded and she began to read aloud:

"Monday. July 16, 1984 – Dear Lord, I just want to tell you what I'm thinking. I'm beginning to realize how important having trust between people is to me. Tom, the guy I was trying to help with a job, stole a couple thousand dollars worth of tools, and headed down the AlCan Highway over the weekend. I just now found out. I've been away since Thursday, and he's probably already in Seattle, or only you know where. I just don't know what to do. Should I file a police report? Or should I let Tom get away with it? I just called Tim now, and told him how much trouble I'm in.

"I told him I have to buy a bunch of new tools to finish this job and I'm already behind schedule and now down a man. God, you say you care in your word. Do you really? I have a wife to take care of, and I'm struggling. So I'm going to claim your promise. Tim gave it to me.

"Trust in him at all times, ye people, Pour out your heart before him. God is your refuge. Psalm 62:8.

Tim also said I could borrow his tools so I could finish this job without going in debt. He said he trusted me, and that I needed to trust you to provide, but that you often work through people. He said he'd help me on his day off if I needed him to."

The journal entry ended abruptly at the end of the page. Laura looked up. "Did he ever tell you about that?"

"No, he didn't." Scott shook his head, "I remember my uncle as always being a successful guy. I had no idea that ever happened." He leaned back. "Of course that was a year before I started working for him, 1984 was the date entry, right? A lot changed since then."

Laura leaned forward and turned a couple more pages. "His next entry isn't until July 27." Her finger followed the line. "You want me to read it?" Scott nodded.

"July 27, 1984 – Dear God, I haven't written here for a while, I have been so busy, but good busy. Thank you so much for helping me get this job done. I finished the framing on Happy Lane with Tim's tools, you know, and I just got my final check. $600. I think I can afford to get more tools now.

"God, you and Tim helped me finish right before the deadline. Thank you for coming through just like Tim said you would. [Of course he helped me frame too!]

"God, I know you know my thoughts, but I want to tell you, since Tim said I should even if you already knew, he said it would help me. So here's what I've been thinking. Tim's been talking about trust an awful lot lately. He said the reason I was struggling with my relationship with you was because of my view of you. That's because of how my dad never cared for me. Tim says I have colored glasses on that say you don't care for me either, since you're my father, too. He said I needed to take off those glasses and smash them up, so that I can see the truth – that you really do have my best interest at heart. It makes me want to be close to you. Strange, because I hate being around my dad.

"God, I feel like you have a purpose for my life, but I don't know what it is. I'm going to start my own business now. ***"Honey, Do Less"*** *finish carpentry and custom home*

remodeling. Tim says I'll do well as long as I follow the principles of trust. And he's given me a boost getting it started too. He says he wants me to know that you care about me in a real tangible way, and you're working through him to do that. Tim says one of the fundamental principles of trust is getting the job done. I guess it's in the Bible. He said this guy saw this starving, cold, naked guy in the street, and said, 'God bless you, be fed, warmed and clothed and depart in peace.' Then turned and walked away without doing anything, leaving the guy the same way he met him. Tim says God isn't like that – he gets the job done. He doesn't just make promises he can't keep. So, to have people trust in my business, I have to get the job done for them too."

Laura folded the book over as the journal entry ended. She noticed Scott's eyes were a little moist. She reached across the table hesitantly and set her hand on top of his. He didn't move away. She squeezed. "You okay, Scott?"

Scott felt his heart do several extra beats when Laura's hand touched his. He had sat listening as she read. The words took him back, and the memory of his uncle and what Matthew had taught him before he had died made him feel like crying. It felt good to have this beautiful woman here with him, and she had just squeezed his hand.

Just then an image of a different girl splashed through his mind. Janet. Instantly Scott's arm tightened, and he unconsciously jerked his hand away from Laura ever so slightly. She noticed and let go of his hand. "I just noticed you were moved by the journal. Are you okay?"

"Ya, I'm fine, just to hear my uncle, and what he tried to teach me. Brings back feelings." Scott swallowed. "Thanks for reading, I appreciate it."

Laura set the journal down. "Why don't we read more later. Let's eat our food and talk about something else for a while."

Scott hadn't even noticed that two baskets of fries and burgers had arrived. He had been too involved in the story to notice the waitress.

Laura took a bite of her burger. "You know, reading that journal made me think." She wiped the corner of her mouth with a napkin. "I guess this might be weird to say." She looked at Scott. "But one of the reasons I'm divorced is because my ex-husband never got the job done. He'd say he was going to do something, and he would never do it. He was fired from almost every job he took. You couldn't depend on him." She picked a French fry. "I soon realized I couldn't trust him with anything." She stopped. "I won't bore you with my drama, though."

"No, no, you're not boring me. I'm interested," Scott responded.

Laura looked up doubtfully. "Well, I'm a nurse now, because when I got divorced, I needed a good job, so I went to night school. I guess you could say desperation made me really good at getting the job done." She stared into her glass and twirled the ice cubes with her straw. "Those where some tough days."

The next hour passed quickly. Laura told Scott about life in Idaho a little and Scott told her about Alaska.

Before they knew it, lunch was over, and Scott was paying the bill. He was quiet on the way back. He seemed to be in the midst of troubled thoughts about what Laura had read. She sensed it and couldn't help but think about it herself.

"So, thanks for the ride and going to lunch with me," Scott said. "I have your number and you have mine. We'll have to hang out again soon." He stood outside of his Uncle John's house, leaning in the truck's window.

"Okay," Laura replied. "I had fun too."

Chapter 7

S cott noticed his aunt's car was parked in the driveway as he closed the gate behind him. It looked like he wasn't alone. He knocked, then opened the front door.

"Hi, Scott, you were gone a while. What did the doctor say about your foot?" Ruth was arranging the pillows on the couch.

"It didn't take hardly any time at all, actually." Scott reached into his pocket and held up the small bottle. "The doctor gave me this ointment to put on every day. I wasn't at the doctor's for more then ten minutes. It was great." Ruth looked up, puzzled. "Oh I went out to lunch with Laura. We drove off base and went to Dina's diner," Scott explained. "Have you been there before? They have great burgers."

"Actually, I never have. I should take John there sometime," she responded. "We don't leave the base all that often. John's work keeps us pretty busy here. It's funny how we live on a tropical island, but we don't hardly get out to do things enough." Ruth laughed. "You'll be hungry for dinner though, won't you?" she asked. "I'm cooking up some tacos."

Scott could smell the aroma of spicy meat and cilantro drifting from the kitchen. "Smells good. I'll be hungry." He sat and took his shoes off. "We actually talked for quite a while after we ate, so I'm already working on a dinner appetite."

"Oh," Ruth said. "So you enjoyed your time with Laura?"

"Yep, actually, I did." He set his shoes on the rug and walked into the living room. "We read in a journal Uncle John gave me yesterday, and talked about Alaska and stuff. She's a really cool girl."

"I see." Ruth was back in the kitchen, stirring peppers on a sizzling pan. Scott stood watching her for a second.

"I'm going to go to my room and read for a while. If there's not anything you need help with," he said.

"Oh sure." She looked up from where she was now chopping an onion. "I'll call for you when John gets home and dinner is ready." She smiled. "Enjoy your reading."

Scott went into his room and closed the door. Flopping out on the bed, he lay thinking about talking with Laura, and Matthew's journal. Time for his mind to catch up.

"I won't read now," he decided.

A few minutes later, John arrived home from the office. He walked into the house and greeted Ruth with a hug and a small kiss.

"I'm still cooking dinner, so why don't you come talk with me in the kitchen?" Ruth said.

"Smells good, don't mind if I do," he responded.

John sat on a barstool while Ruth talked. "Scott didn't get home until just 15 minutes ago. He's in his room reading now."

"Oh really?" John began to sit up alarmed. " Is it serious? The doctor kept him that long?"

"Oh, no, " Ruth held up her paring knife. "He was out talking with Laura at Dina's diner. His foot is healing fine, he told me."

"That's good." John relaxed. "So he's hitting it off well with Laura, then." He picked up a chunk of cheese and popped it in his mouth.

"Yes, he is, and I'm happy about that." Ruth lifted her eyebrows. "But, I'm a little worried, too. I hope I didn't help start something that he can't handle. I don't know if Scott's ready for a relationship."

"Well, I guess we can't worry about it too much. He's twenty-one," John observed. "If Scott learns what I hope he learns from his uncle's journal, I think he'll do okay with her."

Ruth pulled the taco shells from the oven and set them on the bar. "I hope so, dear. Can you go call Scott? The tacos are ready."

Dinner was a pleasant affair. Informal and tasty. Scott wasn't very hungry, but he couldn't help but eat three tacos, despite himself. His aunt knew how to cook. The bar was lined with all the ingredients and they sat on stools in the kitchen talking.

Scott told his uncle what the doctor had said, and a little bit about going to lunch with Laura. He didn't tell that they had read the journal together, though.

John was making another taco, piling sour cream and green sauce onto the top. "That's the thing with tacos," he said. "They don't make the shells big enough for all the good stuff Ruth makes for them. So there's a guy I was talking to in my office today. An Air Force mechanic. I won't tell you his name, just because as a chaplain we maintain confidentiality." John set his taco on his plate and swung his bar stool to face Scott.

"The guy reminded me of myself when I was younger, actually." John's eyes looked reminiscent. "He told me how he was searching for truth, but he didn't know where to look." John took a bite of his taco. "And of course he has some personal issues since he turned his back on God's principles. It took him a while to admit that though." John chuckled.

"Integrity is very important, I wish I could show these young guys better how keeping it would remove so many heartaches." He wiped his mouth with his napkin. "Have you started reading your uncle's journal yet?" He looked at Scott, who nodded.

"Just a little bit. I read about him having his tools stolen, and a few other things."

"Well, if you keep reading, and carefully too, you'll learn three principles about trust. They can change your life if you follow them. I'm not gonna tell you what they are, though." He raised his hand. "You gotta find them yourself." He crunched on the last of his taco and stood and walked to the sink, carrying his plate. "When you've found them, why don't you come tell me, and we'll see what we can learn from each other?" John rinsed his plate and set it in the dish rack. "Great tacos, honey. Why don't I start on these dishes, and we can all go and play some dominoes after dinner is done?"

*****

After playing a couple of runs of "Mexican train" with John and Ruth, Scott politely excused himself. "I'm going to see if I can find those principles of trust you where talking about, Uncle John. I bet I can find them before the night's over." Scott stood from the table.

"Tell me when you find them." John chuckled. "But don't stress about it, they'll come if you just let the journal flow."

Back in his room, Scott shut the door and lay out on the bed, propped himself on his elbows, and took a deep breath. Time to really get into this thing.

He flipped the journal open and flicked past the first pages.

August 10, 1987, was the next entry.

I finally started my own business, I don't know what to expect, but I'm excited. I got a contract to do framing with

*some guys in Anchorage working on new construction. Will
see how things go. Got to get some sleep it's getting late.*

The line ended abruptly. *I wonder when I come into this
picture?* Scott thought. It was at the end of that summer his
uncle had first hired Scott to work for him.

Scott thought back. He had been bumming around home
that August, irritated with his dad who was always trying
to analyze and teach him. His dad had been critical of his
brother-in-law, telling Scott how he didn't have it together.
He claimed that he, the psychotherapist, could have fixed all
the problems of his brother-in-law if he only listened to him
and not Timothy . It was the same thing he told Scott, so the
fact that his dad didn't approve of Matthew only increased
Scott's admiration for him.

His uncle had started his business that summer and he
offered Scott a job towards the end of that August.

Scott turned the page. It was like he was re-viewing the
whole thing through his uncle's eyes now.

*August 29,1987 – My brother-in-law, Robert, has never
approved of me. I think that he doesn't agree with my new
Christian beliefs and thinks I'm too simple. Can't help that
much. I met his family the other day. He and his oldest son,
Phillip, seem a lot alike. He's grooming Phillip to go to
college and work with him in his practice. His wife seems
reserved and didn't show too much personality. She seems
to just agree with whatever her husband said, They have a
younger son, but he's different. His name's Scott. I can't help
but like the guy. He's the underdog, and his dad is always on
him, but he still seems to have a spark in him—*

*August 30,1987—Today I asked Scott if he wanted
to work with me. He said he wanted to get away from his
house and earn some money, so we agreed. So, now I have
my first "Employee." And he's my brother-in-law's son! At
first I didn't think Robert would let him, but he shrugged
his shoulders, and said it would be "better then having him*

around there." On to other things. My wife and I found a "new" place to rent in Anchorage. So we are getting more settled. Tim says I have a good opportunity, working with my nephew. That I can make a big difference in his life too.

Scott bent forward, his eyes focusing on the page.

—Scott's 15. He seems to be a very angry young man, though he probably thinks he hides it very well. I suppose as long as I don't push his buttons like his dad does, he'll be a good employee. I think he has a lot of potential.

Reading about these events put Scott into a dark place emotionally. He didn't see how this would give him the principles of trust. But he wanted to answer his uncle's challenge, so he continued reading.

September 1, 1987. Brrr. It sure is getting cold, but the work is good. I was worried that I couldn't find any, because Alaska is just coming out of an economic crash, but Tim has given me recommendations so I have not suffered from it.

September 19, 1987. My wife and I have had some disagreements. She is angry at me for working so much, and thinks I don't listen to her. I don't know what to do. I do listen, but I don't think she notices. If I don't work, I can't pay the bills. I do love her dearly though.

Hopefully I won't have to work so much soon, life is getting more routine, and Scott is becoming a big help. I taught him how to frame and he's an iron man. I like being able to pay him big bonuses, like I just did. He helped me get a job done almost a week early. I'm glad he's going back to school for his sake, but for mine I'll miss the guy. He's fun to be around.

I think God has really blessed my business, I keep on getting recommended to new jobs and I'm only limited by myself. I think I should try to hire a couple of hands, and then maybe I can find more time to work on my marriage, and just supervise. Today I was talking with Timothy and he say's I have a talent for leading, and he's very pleased with how I've helped Scott. I think it's probably the first time he's ever really felt good about himself.

Scott stopped reading to readjust a pillow underneath him.

September 21, 1987. Scott went back to school today. Now he can only work part-time. He told me plain out that he didn't want to go to school. I definitely need to hire some help now. I didn't realize how much of a help he was until now, and the work just keeps coming.

I went to lunch with Timothy today. I hadn't talked with him for almost a week now. I told him about my wife and asked for prayer. I also told him I wanted to hire some new guys to work with me.

We talked and there are two principles he said I needed. Number 1, getting the job done. He said as long as I did the job and did it well, I would do well in construction. He also said that I needed to get the job done for my wife, and if that meant spending time with her, I needed to make the time.

And number 2, I need to have integrity, If I run my business with integrity, and am honest, I will do well. I also need to have integrity with my wife, and be honest and good to her.

So I am making a mental note that I will have integrity in my business, and I will get the job done!

Scott read the journal, every page up through December, pouring over every page. He only stopped twice to rearrange himself and finally to sit on the floor and lean his back against the bed.

January 1ˢᵗ, 1988. I finally figured it out! I know what I've been missing out on! It's having other people's best interest in mind. I can't believe I missed it. These last months have been busy and my business has grown to the point that I have three guys who work for me regularly now, but I've lost several key contracts that I was sure I'd have, and I've been wracking my brain, trying to figure out why. I empha-size heavily on having integrity with the guys, and we always have gotten the jobs done on time, but it just dawned on me. I've been losing customers because I haven't had their best interest at heart. My marriage has been suffering because I don't have my wife's best interest at heart, even though I always have integrity and have been faithful to her... I suddenly get it! That's why I have been losing so many relationships.

So I talked with Timothy about it, and he kinda gently helped me discover what I was missing. It's so wonderful to have a pastor mentor like him. Who knows where I'd be if it wasn't for Timothy?

I've also been mentoring my nephew, Scott, even though he probably doesn't realize it. We've gotten closer recently. He's opened up to me about how his dad is so hard on him. It's been very frustrating, because whenever I teach Scott a Christian principle, like having integrity or something, my brother-in-law tells him how stupid it is, and to learn some real psychology. That's difficult.

January 4th 1988. My wife scares me right now. She's been reading some new self-help books she got from her brother. She tells me they really focus on expressing yourself and how every feeling we have as humans is good. She even went so far as to tell me yesterday that people can tap into the universe and become like God, and there really isn't a right and wrong, strictly speaking. We've been clashing a lot about that. Whenever I read something from the Bible, she gets angry at me. Our views are really clashing, but yet I can't tell her that she's wrong. Maybe I'm in the wrong. I don't know...

Scott closed the book. *I think I have the answer now. I'll go see what John says.*

He moved out of the bedroom and down the hall. John sat in an easy chair reading a book. "John," Scott said, "I think I found those three principles."

John set his book down and looked up over the rims of his glasses. "You've been reading this whole time?" He glanced at the clock. "It's almost 10 PM."

"I think they're having integrity, getting the job done, and having people's best interest in mind." Scott counted them off on his fingers and looked hesitantly at John. "Am I right?"

"Good job, good job." John rose from his chair. "Scott, I want you to come see something." He walked across the wooden floor and down the hall. Scott followed. "This is my study, and part time junk room." He motioned to Scott to have a seat on a wooden stool on the floor. "I have studied and read several books on trust," he said quietly. "And these last years since my brother's death, I've studied every verse on trust I can find in the Bible. His journal helped me discover what I now know. The Bible says a lot about trust, but boiled down, it comes to three main principles. Can I see that stool you're sitting on?"

Scott stood up, uncertain, and handed the stool to his uncle. John held it up.

"See, it has three legs." He jiggled one leg until it popped out. "Sit on this." He handed the chair back to Scott.

Scott sat unevenly on the chair, but after a second he found his balance and managed to stop swaying.

"You're sitting how a lot of people are," John said. "You can trust them pretty well in two areas, like if they get the job done and have integrity. But then something comes along where they have to choose between themselves and your best interest, and you know what happens?"

Scott shook his head. John stepped forward and gave him a gentle shove. The stool fell from under him and he tumbled to the carpet.

"That's what happens." John reached out a hand. "Let me help you up. You want to try it again?" he asked, laughing. "Only this time with one leg?"

Scott shook his head. "I think I already know what will happen."

John laughed. "That's right. You may not even be able to balance, even without a shove." John twisted the leg back into the stool's seat. "Try it now."

Scott sat on the stool with all three legs, and John gave him the same gentle push. This time he only slightly rocked.

"You see, to truly be trustworthy, you have to have all three legs of trust," John said. "Most people usually are weak in at least one area." He shrugged. "I'll leave that for you to think about. If you find out where you're weak, then you can improve and life will get much better for you."

"I think I know," said Scott. "Kinda like this guy named Tony in Ebi. He was really good at getting the job done, and okay at integrity with most things. But he was so selfish, you couldn't trust him."

"Didn't have your best interest in mind." John nodded. "Or how about this, you have a friend who wants to help you get money because you need it, and always follows through? So he's good at getting the job done, and he wants to help you, so he has your best interest at heart." John paused. "So he says, 'Let's rob a bank.' See, he doesn't have integrity so he's going to get you hurt."

Scott nodded. "I see."

John raised his hand. "Now that's an extreme example, but I wanted to make a contrast. Nobody can ever completely trust you unless you have all three. The only one who will only ever have the three legs of trust completely is God. He has your best interest at heart, he gets the job done and comes through a hundred percent of the time, and he has perfect integrity." John leaned back, "I'll get off my soapbox now." He winked and gave Scott a friendly slap on the back. "Your probably tired, I'm sure…"

*****

Scott lay in bed that night, wondering. He kept going over and over the journal and what his uncle had said in his mind, until he fell into a troubled sleep.

Chapter 8

The morning sun broke through the curtains. Scott rose quickly from the blankets and rubbed his head. He had dreamed of Tony. He had been running behind him, chasing him down a white beach with a three-legged stool.

He had just dressed and walked out when he heard the phone ring. He heard Ruth answer it.

"Oh, yes I'll see if Scott's awake, hold on." A second later, she stuck her head around the corner. "Oh, there you are, Scott. Laura's on the phone for you."

Scott walked to the phone and lifted it to his ear. "Hello?"

Laura's voice was lively. "Hey, you early bird, It's already 9:00."

"Well I was up last night…" Scott paused. "…reading the journal, so I have a good excuse."

Laura laughed. "That's why I'm calling. I was wondering if you want to get together and read some more."

Scott paused a second. "Sure, what time?" He tried to sound nonchalant.

"How about lunch again? That will give you time to get your beauty sleep in."

"Hey! I need my beauty sleep. We aren't all born equal!" He protested.

"Okay I'll see you then." Laura laughed. "Bye."

He heard the phone click, and Scott turned away from the phone.

In the kitchen he joined his Aunt Ruth for cheerios and fresh bananas.

"So you're going out again today?" Ruth was slicing a banana into her bowl.

"Yes, for lunch," he responded. "We've been reading through Matthew's journal together."

Ruth lifted her eyes. "How's that going?"

"Good." He obviously wasn't giving enough information because Ruth probed further.

"So would you consider Laura to be a 'special friend.'" She pronounced the 'special' with a little lift at the end.

"Why in the world would you think that?" Scott feigned surprise, then grew serious. "I don't think so. We're just friends, I think. I'm only going to be here for a little while anyways." He shook his head again. "Just friends."

Ruth grew serious. "Just be careful," she warned. "I know John talked to you about the three legs of trust last night, so just make sure you keep them all with her, and don't give her an impression that isn't true." She laughed and flicked a Cheerio at Scott. "I'm just looking out for us girls, because you are just a fun, good looking guy, and I don't want Laura to be hopelessly in love with you if you don't feel the same."

He laughed. "Don't worry about that." But he thought about what she said.

Later that morning, Scott wasn't quite sure about the "just friends" thing. Ruth had gone to work, and left him in the quiet house, still an hour before Laura was picking him up.

Maybe he was giving the wrong message. He thought about it and realized he was having mixed feelings himself. She was gorgeous, he couldn't ignore that fact. Not that that was enough, but he had been having a lot of fun with her, too. Her bubbly teasing put him at ease. He hadn't enjoyed talking to someone like her for a long time. He knew that for a fact.

But then Scott thought back to Janet, No, no one could replace her. He would remain single forever! He shook his head. He needed to stop thinking about Laura. How ridiculous was that, anyways? She lived in Idaho and he in Alaska and he was leaving really soon. He shook his head, but the image of her smiling face and dark hair made him shake his head in frustration.

"Stop brain! Stop!" Scott banged his head. "You're just lonely and confused, get yourself under control, don't let what Ruth said get you all wound up," he ordered himself.

Laura arrived right on time, 12:30. She didn't help erase Scott's opinion about how beautiful she was, either. When she stepped out of her truck in a cute green shirt and black shorts, she waved cheerily to him. Scott had hoped she wouldn't see him standing there in the window, mouth agape, staring dumbly.

"What am I doing?" He turned and pinched himself. "Get yourself together."

He met her at the door. "Let me grab the journal, come right in." Scott beckoned. "I'll be right back." He turned and went down the hall, to return a moment later. "Let's go!"

"Why don't we try something new and exciting today?" Laura asked. "We could try driving to the beach somewhere and finding a fun place to eat."

"Okay." He nodded.

"How's your foot doing, by the way?" She glanced across the truck at Scott's shoe.

"Oh, it's healing well, all closed up now. That cream's doing magic. I think I'll give it another day, and I'll be good for swimming and sandals again."

"Be careful" Laura steered the truck around a corner. "That foot has given you too much trouble already." She headed for the airbase gate.

Before too long, they were driving through a lively little tourist section. Beach clubs, restaurants, and people walking, shopping in an open-air market.

"This looks like a good spot." Laura pulled the truck off into a café parking lot. "Why don't we find a good little restaurant here and explore a little bit?

They walked down the road and through a market. There were t-shirts, shells and colorful knickknacks spread out underneath a frond gazebo. Fresh mangos, pineapple and avocados where stacked in wooden boxes. Persistent vendors waved and beckoned.

"Let's go there." Laura pointed. They made their way to a wooden patio overlooking the beach. Several food stands sold ice cream, hotdogs, burgers, lemonade, and fish and chips. Surfers and sun bathers stood in a few lines, and others sat licking ice cream cones and reading magazines.

After ordering a couple of hotdogs, Scott found a table under the shade of a palm tree. It was right on the edge of the deck, overlooking the surf breaking across the sandy white beach.

"Nice spot." Laura sat across from Scott. "Doesn't it make you just want to go grab a board right now and paddle out?"

"It looks fun. We should do something like that." Scott was watching two buff guys paddling surfboards out into the green water.

"So you've read more of the journal, what did I miss?" Laura was rustling through the pages of the journal.

Scott told her what he had read, and then about the three legs of trust and how John had given him an analogy of it.

"I was really thinking about what my uncle said to me and I realized what my biggest weakness was," he confided. "I struggle with getting the job done." He shifted, feeling a little self-conscious. "I mean, I get things down, but I'm such an entrepreneur that I start way too many projects, get discouraged on them, and don't finish what I start." He paused and looked over the crashing waves for a long moment. "I've lost trust with several people because I'll get really excited about something, say a new business idea, and talk them all up about it. Then a few months later, when nothing happens, they lose trust in me." Scott rapped his fingers on the plastic table. "I really need to stop that." He shook his head.

Laura looked thoughtful. "It's hard for me to admit this, but I think I struggle a lot with that last one your uncle discovered." She paused. "What was it? Having peoples best interest at heart?" Scott nodded. "That's it." Laura bit her lip, "I think I'm pretty good at getting the job done, but I'm such a bulldog." She shook her head. "I've hurt a lot of people while I'm doing things. That sure has made nursing harder." She laughed. "The turf wars with other pissed-off hospital staff. You don't want to hear about them, it's ugly business." Laura looked thoughtful. "I'm struggling because I think I pride myself on the fact that I'm so calloused. I mean, you need to be when you're a nurse." She seemed to be arguing with herself. "Though I think it's good to be able to stand up for myself, I need to be more sensitive to the needs of people around me." She nodded. "It's hard for me to admit, but I think people could trust me a lot more if I did."

The two sat in silence, deep in thought. The wind rustled the palm fronds above them and the incessant screaming of gulls over the crash of breakers made a dim canopy of noise behind them.

"Intense stuff," he said. "It's hard to change sometimes."

Laura nodded. "Why don't we read some more of the journal?"

"Okay." Scott reached over and leafed through the pages. "This is where I stopped. I read all the way up to January 1988, it looks like."

"Aw, I'm missing Christmas?" Laura pretended to pout.

"He actually didn't talk too much about Christmas, more about worrying about work, and learning about God and how to be trusted and stuff like that."

"I'm joking." Laura gave Scott a mischievous look. "I can go over and read it later. Do you want me to read?"

He nodded. "Go ahead."

Laura began. "January 4, 1988. My wife scares me right now. She's been reading some new self-help books she got from her brother. She tells me they really focus on expressing yourself and how every feeling we have as humans is good. She even went so far as to tell me yesterday that people can tap into the universe and become like God, and there really isn't a right and wrong, strictly speaking. We've been clashing a lot about that. Whenever I read something from the Bible, she gets angry at me. Our views are really clashing, but yet I can't tell her that she's wrong. Maybe I'm in the wrong. I don't know…"

"Hmm..." Scott fiddled with a plastic fork. "It sounds like he was having a few marital issues." He remembered that things had seemed a little bit strained those last few months, Matthew had been tight-lipped and very focused on work, and had not been near as jovial as he had before. He hadn't said much to Scott other than that he had a few 'Personal issues' he needed to work out with Aunt Tiff.

"You ready for the next one?" Laura looked at Scott questioningly.

"Sure." Scott nodded.

"January 29, 1988. I hired a new foreman today. His name's Owen, an old friend of Robert. He say's he's really dependable. I think this is a good move, because now I won't have to spend so much time managing and doing paper work and I can spend more time doing the things I'm good at and working on my marriage. Thank you, God, for that!

"My nephew, Scott, is working with me part-time after school. He can actually accomplish more in four hours after

school than some of my guys can working all day. I think when he's out of school I'll give him a supervisor position, if he still wants to work for me. My only worry is that he's too young and they won't listen to him. He is pretty cocky, too, but we're working on that. I've been telling him about having integrity and following Christ, and he seems to be listening. Sometimes I just don't know. I'm giving advice and people are listening to me now, but inside my own marriage things are out of control. I don't know how to deal with my wife when she's so furious about me studying the Bible with Tim, and trying to undermine and prove everything I believe in is wrong. I don't know if I have the right to give Scott advice. God please help my marriage.—

"February 16, 1988. I feel really uncomfortable. Maybe I'm just being overly sensitive and overreacting. — I'm writing so I can figure it out. –Today I invited my foreman over for dinner with my wife and me. He's really been helping me get things under control at work, so I wanted to introduce him to me and my wife a little bit more — but this is what happened. After dinner when we were eating dessert, we started talking about God, and he told me he was really big into the New Age movement and that I was off base — he told me that kindly, of course, because I'm his boss, but my wife picked up on that right away and just began to tear into me. I felt so humiliated. She sided with him and was really friendly to him and treated me like dirt. Maybe I'm overreacting. I need to think, but God, I'm feeling this really strongly. Please help me see the truth—"

Laura shook her head as the reading ended. "That's awful," she muttered. "When I see married people trash each other in front of other people, I think it's about the most hurtful thing."

"Definitely doesn't have the three legs of trust." Scott chimed in.

"You've been picking up on that, haven't you?" Laura laughed. "Of course I'm trying to be impartial here. There's two sides to every story."

Scott nodded. "I never got along with Owen anyways, though, and you know she's married to that foreman now."

"No way." Laura gasped.

"Yep." Scott nodded. "Just three weeks after Matthew's accident, she married him."

"That's so wrong," Laura fumed.

"Lets keep reading."

There where several more entries about work and the continuing drama with Matthew's wife. He also talked about studying with Tim, how frustrated he was with how stubborn all his relatives were about accepting Christ, and how Scott seemed to be the only one who would listen.

"June 17, 1988 – Summer is in full swing now and the building season here in Alaska is quickening. The demand is great because everyone and their brother is trying to get things framed and roofed before winter. It seems word of mouth over the winter has spread that I'm a good contractor, and I'm having to turn down work now. When the big crash happened a few years ago, a lot of the construction workers left and now there's more than enough work for us who are here. Scott's working for me now. He's out of school and I have him supervising two other young summer helpers I just hired. He's doing great, and making a pile of money. I let him have several fun, easy jobs, because I have so many to choose from and I like helping him out. It feels good to help someone else become successful. Payroll is coming up, I don't have much time to write now. I need to go talk with Owen.

"June 22, 1988. I'm worried right now. Owen, my foreman, has been doing most of the paperwork for me, because I hate it so much. I'm not that good with numbers anyways, but it seems like things aren't quite right with the

end of the month report he just gave me. He just bought a brand new truck, too. Maybe I'm being paranoid. He gave some big expense reports for building materials on several jobs, and I asked Scott and he doesn't think materials could have been more then $7,000 on this new garage he built for a client, but Owen put down $13,000 and has receipts to prove it. He bought twice as much lumber as we needed, and no one seems to know where it went. Scott told me that one of his guys overheard that Owen is friends with a guy who's remodeling a house in Anchorage and that he overheard him say that "he had some extra materials he could give him for a good discount." But it's just too hard to say.

"And what's extra hard is that Owen is on really good standing with my brother-in-law since they are high school buddies, and it would be a very political thing for me if I confronted him about it. I just need to not get paranoid and just make sure I'm not jumping to conclusions."

"I remember that." Scott nodded. "I thought Owen was a snake and I'm still of the same opinion."

"Do you think he really stole that lumber?" Laura asked.

"I can't say, but it sure disappeared into thin air." Scott shrugged.

Laura continued reading. "July 2, 1988. I'm getting really upset with my foreman and I think he knows it. He doesn't seem to be worried about it, though. He's been late for work several times, too. Yesterday, I needed a nail gun I had left in my garage, and he said he would stop and grab it while he swung by the hardware store. He didn't get back for two hours, and then he left for the hardware store! When I got home, my wife seemed very distant and when I asked her if he had stopped by, she got really defensive and angry. I stopped, not wanting to go any further, but I'm worried… I wish I could fire him and hire Scott to be my foreman. He may not have as much experience, but at least I can trust him!

"July 4,1988. Today we had a family picnic, the whole works: watermelon, hotdogs, baked beans, potato chips. Unknown to me, my brother-in-law invited Owen, my foreman. I of course had to play along, not showing that I hadn't wanted him to come. My brother-in-law was talking with him like he owned the company. It makes me wonder just how close Robert and Owen are to each other?! I felt very put out, like they are in a small gang together and they both don't like me ... I'm very frustrated with how things are going. I don't know how I got into this mess. It's making me jumpy. I need to confront my foreman about the money that keeps disappearing, but I think I'll wait until I've given him enough rope to hang himself.

"July 27, 1988. I have a horrible reality. I almost don't want to think about it! I think my foreman is having an affair with my wife. She denies it, saying he's only a friend, but things have never been so strained between me and her. I am just trying to keep my head in my work, and praying hard. I talked with Tim about my fears for the first time yesterday. He seemed very worried. He says he'll pray hard, and he believes I need to confront Owen about it. I told him I was going to wait until I had grounds to fire him, and there was no way he could deny it. He's really foxy, he can talk his way out of anything and I am too straightforward to have a battle of wits with him. I think he knows the position I'm in with my wife and her brother, so he's been very arrogant. Almost challenging to me.

"August 10, 1988. I'm going to challenge Owen tomorrow. I think I finally have enough evidence that he can't deny it. I need your help so much, God. My company is working on framing the roof on a four-story apartment building. I will have to inspect the site with Owen after the work is done, and I believe that will be a good time to confront him. I am sure almost $10,000 worth of materials are missing from the jobsite, so I'll bring my receipt ledger which he gave me. I'll

ask him where the material is, then I will confront him about the other materials and fire him if he cannot show me positively within a short period of time where all of it is.

"I sent Scott to work on a different job, not wanting him to be around when this all goes down. I love my family and I love God, I just want everything to work out for good..."

The journal ended. Laura flipped pages, but they were all empty. "What happened? Why did it end?"

Scott cleared his throat. "That was my uncle's last journal entry because he..." Scott's faced flashed—all the pieces were coming together. "...before he died." Scott suddenly shot up from his chair. "The foreman must have murdered Matthew!" He yelled it, and then sat back down in the chair, pulse racing. Could it be true?

"I always suspected something was up between Aunt Tiff and Owen, but I never had thought..." Scott's voice broke. "... that my uncle had died of anything other than an accident."

Laura looked confused at Scott's sudden outburst. "I don't understand."

Scott's face was set in a hard line. "The official accident report was that Matthew was knocked of the roof by a sliding piece of plywood, and that a skill saw slid off with him and fell and hit him across his forehead. He died from the impact along with massive bleeding."

Scott flashed back. He could remember that day like it was happening now. He had no idea of what he now knew, only that his uncle had a few marital issues — didn't everyone? — and that perhaps the foreman was a little dishonest, though he always got the job done. Matthew had seemed very quiet and focused on work, but Scott had just figured that it was from the stress of managing three different construction sites.

He had been framing with one other guy at another job-site that August 11th when his dad drove up in his truck. Tight-lipped, and white-knuckled.

"Get in the car son," he had ordered.

A horrible accident had happened, Uncle Matthew was in the hospital, and no one knew if he'd live. Scott remembered being in the ER room, seeing his aunt sobbing and his mom trying to comfort her, and then being told that his uncle was dead. It had been the worst day of Scott's life.

"Scott, why don't we go for a walk?" Laura gently touched Scott on the arm. "Let's walk down the beach and talk about it."

He stood and followed Laura shakily down toward the blue-green water, clutching the journal in his hand.

Laura asked him to tell her, so he did. He told her how he had been told of his uncle's death, and then how the foreman had taken over the business. Owen had married Tiff within three weeks of Matthew's death and, of course, Scott's dad had thought it was a good idea.

When Scott heard the announcement that Owen was going to marry Tiff, he had resigned from working at the company.

"That's when I started my own handyman business. Several of the guys resigned with me right then, too."

The waves where washing up around their feet.

"So how did you get out here to the islands?" Laura looked up at Scott, her big brown eyes softening.

"After I started my own company, my aunt gave me a whole bunch of New Age books, and told me they were Matthew's and that he would have wanted me to have them. I couldn't believe it, though. All the books seemed brand new. I started reading them, though." Scott shuddered and shook his head. "Bad idea. When I started believing what those books said, and turning away from God, my life went from bad to worse. I was in a very dark, depressed place." He looked away. "I don't really like to talk about it." He cleared his throat, "Anyways, after a while, Timothy, the pastor Matthew wrote about in his journal, contacted me. Long story short, I started studying the Bible with him, and then I found out about a mission in the Marshall Islands that needed teachers. Things were bad at home, and I wanted to go somewhere where I could grow and get away from all the old influences, so I came. And you know the rest of the story."

The two walked side-by-side. Laura's hand brushed lightly against Scott's.

"I'm dreading going back worse than anything now." Scott was looking down. "Especially now that I suspect there may have been some foul play. I don't know if I can face Owen." He kicked at the sand. "I need to talk to John. He knows more about it than me," Scott reasoned with himself. "Why don't we walk up to that market? I need to get my mind off of this."

"Okay" Laura turned with Scott and led the way up to a fish market.

*****

"I want to go snorkeling while I'm here, to get my mind off of Matthew." Scott looked at a colorful calendar of Guam that had vivid depictions of vibrant reefs. "My Uncle John has gear, and he'll let us borrow it. You want to go?"

"Sure," Laura responded. "But where should we? This is my first time to Guam."

"We need to find a local who can tell us. How about that place right there? Paradise Snorkeling?" He pointed to a small wooden hut decked with pictures of colorful fish. A dark native man sat inside. "He'll know."

Scott walked up to the stand. "Excuse me, but do you know where the good beach snorkeling is around here?"

The man brightened behind the counter. "Of course," he said. "I'll tell you, but I must warn you I'm partial to my charter!" He laughed. "I love the reef, though, and I would love to tell you where the good stuff is." He paused and looked to Laura. "What are you guys looking for?"

"What type of places are there?" Laura asked.

"Well one easy favorite is a place called the 'Graveyard,'" the native explained. "No, no it isn't a bad place, but there's a whole bunch of tanks from World War II that sank there. He laughed again. "Not dangerous. People love it, because a reef is growing there, and there's lots of pretty fish." He looked at Laura and Scott. "Let me give you a map of several good spots and also our charter prices." He handed Scott a paper. "We're having a trip to the Graveyard tomorrow. We leave here at noon and it's $20 a person."

"Thank you, We'll talk it over." Scott shook the man's hand, then turned and walked down the street with Laura. "I don't want to go with a charter." Scott read the pamphlet carefully. "It says here it's accessible from the beach. Why don't we leave real early tomorrow and beat the rush?"

After a little bit more planning, Laura agreed. "Well do it tomorrow then, bright and early."

Chapter 9

Scott was up early, even before John. All night Scott had been waking to check the time, glancing at the iridescent numbers on the clock next to the bed. The night couldn't have passed slower, because today was the day that Laura and he where going to Nimitz Beach.

The night before, he had talked Laura into going. A local guide had recommended Nimitz Beach, along with a popular wreck nicknamed "the shark pit," and the WWII memorial there.

This morning, Scott was taking his uncle's truck to pick up Laura. He had told her to be ready at 7 AM. Scott had borrowed a mask and snorkels from John, and had a cooler with a packed lunch from Ruth. He was set.

Scott waved from the little white pickup as he backed out of the driveway.

"Have fun and be careful. Know your limits in the ocean," John had warned him as he tossed the rubber flippers in the truck bed.

"I'll be fine," Scott had replied flippantly. Didn't his uncle know he had just come from the Marshall Islands? He shook his head as he steered the truck away. *I know what I'm doing,* he thought.

The night before, his uncle had been a little unsure when Scott asked him what he thought of the snorkeling outing, but once Scott had explained the area and told him how well his foot had healed, John had given him the thumbs up.

"You're a man now, Scott. I trust you to know what's best for you. All the gear's in my shed." He handed Scott the key.

Scott was whistling a merry tune as he pulled up at Charles's apartment.

"Bright-eyed and bushy-tailed?" Scott asked, as Laura emerged from the house.

She was brushing her dark hair with one hand, while she held her beach bag with the other. A couple of plump mangos poked from the side pocket.

"I'm on vacation, I'm not supposed to be getting up this early except for work," Laura complained good naturedly.

"The tide doesn't know you're on vacation," Scott said.

"Want some mango?" Laura sat down next to him.

"Now that's worth getting up for."

She laughed.

Twenty minutes later, they arrived at Orate Point, Scott parked the truck and the two strolled along through the old World War II memorial with their beach bags.

"Look at that pillbox." Scott pointed at an old concrete bunker. A plaque marked it as a Japanese fortification.

"Wouldn't have wanted to be here 40 years ago." Laura laughed.

They walked up to Orate Point and looked out across the bay, then strolled back by the war memorial and down the beach toward the Agate Cemetery Wall.

The waves washed up gently onto the white sand, and rolled smoothly back.

"Looks like a perfect day for a swim." Scott surveyed the horizon of the morning ocean.

A gull flew overhead screeching, and the green jungle contrasted nicely with the white sand. "Lets get behind the cemetery wall, and walk out as far as we can."

Scott stopped to explain the plan to an attentive Laura. They were going to walk out along the coral wall as far as they could, then have a pleasant swim across the reef area strewn with old tanks and jeeps, which now had coral and sea fans growing on them.

"It's called the shark pit because you'll occasionally see a reef shark. Just like the guide said, nothing to be afraid of."

They found a place where they could stash their bag in some tall jungle grass along the beach. Laura slipped out of her T-shirt and into an attractive bathing suit, then helped Scott get the rubber fins and mask ready.

"Okay, then." Scott kicked sand toward Laura and ran up the beach, with her following close behind.

"Hey Scott, your foot's going to be okay on the coral?"

Scott's feet made little sandy marks ahead of her. His right foot looked white and still she could see the wound's healing scar.

"Oh yeah," Scott said. "See? It's healing up nicely." He stopped, then held his foot up for her to see; the wound had closed and a thin layer of new skin covered the scar. "I'll be wearing flippers, so I won't be totally barefoot. I'll be fine."

As soon as they reached the end of the spit, Scott dove into the warm water enthusiastically. He surfaced and bounced on the sandy bottom while he pulled his flippers over his feet. Laura already had hers on when Scott glanced sideways to look for her.

"Let's go, slowpoke," she teased.

That's it. I'll show her who's the slowpoke! Scott thought. He turned and kicked toward her, plowing his face into the water. He was surprised at himself, He didn't seem to go as fast as he had remembered. And he had to slow before he hardly had started.

"I was just joking." Laura had slowed and was waiting for Scott. "I was on my high school swim team, so it's not really fair."

Scott glanced down in the water at her well-toned legs, which moved below the clear water. She was the epitome of fit, and she was very calm and relaxed; definitely not a panicky land lubber. He tried not to pant.

"I'm not my normal self. I think those days in the hospital and being sick weakened me." He paused to breathe, treading water, "I used to be able to do stuff like this without even getting winded at all."

"We'll just take it easy, then. There's no hurry." Laura smiled.

Scott nodded and stuck his head down in the water. *That's what I usually would tell the new girls on Ebi,* he thought. It was humbling to be on the slow end. They paddled slowly, side by side, until the sand began to drop off a little deeper, and coral and sea grass began to appear. A couple of minutes later, Laura nudged Scott, pointing a hand toward a metal object. An old tank looked up at them from the bottom, its barrel pointed skyward. It was half-buried in the sand, and had little yellow fish darting around it.

"How'd that get out here?" Laura raised her head from the water.

Scott was treading water next to her, peering down. "This is what happened..." He felt smart knowing. "When the Americans landed here, they equipped some of their tanks with what they called a 'skirt,' which was basically a float that made the tank more buoyant and the tanks had little propellers that drove them to the beach. They didn't always work, as you can see."

As they paddled further, they could see old Jeeps and landing vehicles in various stages of decay, littering the sand and coral. A school of tuna swam below.

"Those sure are big fish." Laura pointed. Through the coral, the school of fish parted and a reef shark swam lazily through its middle. Laura reached up and clutched Scott's wrist. "Shark."

"It's okay." Scott blew the water out of his tube. "He's just a little white tip. I saw 8-9 foot reef sharks in the Marshall's all the time, and they never bothered me."

Laura calmed and they both resumed snorkeling, watching the shark circle slowly.

"They really are beautiful." Scott stuck his head above water. "They usually hunt at night, so it's kinda unusual to see them during the day like this."

They continued to watch the shark until it swam deeper out of sight. Scott lifted his head from the water again. The sound of a boat's motor caused him to look toward shore. Several speedboats crowded with snorkelers were bouncing out toward them. Scott made out the lettering on the boats as they neared. Paradise Snorkeling was printed on the sides of all three boats.

"Ahh, here comes that snorkeling charter," Scott grumbled to Laura. "They'll scare all the fish away."

"I still see fish," Laura said.

One of the boats pulled up next to them, and curious faces peered over at them, tourists rubbing themselves with sunscreen. The guide looked down at them as Scott gripped the side of the boat.

"How's the snorkeling?" he asked.

"Ahhh, just swam out from Agate Point, haven't seen everything yet." Scott lifted his snorkel and rubbed his face.

The guide laughed. "Good man, good man."

"We just saw a little reef shark a while ago," Laura said. "It was so cool."

A excited murmur rose from the boat crowded with first time snorkelers.

"Shark? Oh, that's way cool," the guide was saying. He turned to the people in the boat. "Reef sharks aren't dangerous, we're very happy when we see them." He gave a little lecture on how some sharks weren't dangerous, and then pulled away after a friendly wave to Scott and Laura. A minute later, the boats begin to spill their snorkelers in little buoy-guided swimmer trains, all wearing life jackets.

"Let's paddle out a little further," Scott said, "so we don't get mixed up with them, and see what out there."

"You're not tired?" Laura asked. Scott shook his head. "Just checking. I'm good if you are, but not too far out. I don't want to push my limits."

They swam out. The water was clear for close to 100 feet in all directions, so they could see the beautiful coral and sand below, along with schools of tuna and other fish. Laura raised her head.

"Guam sits at the top of the Marianas Trench, the world's deepest ocean site. It's kinda like diving the world's tallest mountain." She splashed playfully at Scott. "Isn't it cool out here?"

I didn't even know that! Scott thought. This girl knew her stuff.

"Lets go out a little further. I want to take a look at that brain coral." Scott pointed, bubbling the words through his snorkel. He kicked ahead of Laura. The giant brain coral fascinated him. He suddenly felt Laura pulling on his flipper. He turned around and raised his head.

"Shark," Laura said. "Over there."

He put his head into the water and looked. Sure enough, about 50 feet away, a gray reef shark was cruising. Not far behind it, another one swam up from the misty blue to join him. They paid no attention to Scott or Laura. Scott knew from experience that gray reef sharks could be aggressive, but these were off minding their own business, and they didn't look to be more than five feet long.

I'll just swim to that brain coral and we'll head back, Scott thought. *This has been an awesome swim.*

Laura was watching the sharks and Scott was only a couple of feet ahead of her. He dove down, kicking to the large round brain coral. It looked big and smooth, like a big golf ball sitting in the reef. Scott turned and his flipper caught in a piece of fire coral. He twisted his foot with annoyance and kicked for the surface. Halfway up, he noticed a peculiar stinging feeling on his foot. He bit his lip. Somehow his foot twisting had reopened his wound. Through his flipper, he could feel the sting of seawater entering it. He breathed and then looked down at his foot. A small smudge of red lifted from under the blue rubber and disappeared into the water. Scott groaned to himself.

He lifted his head. Laura was pulling his arm. "Scott, there are more sharks swimming over there."

Scott lowered his head down and peered where the first two had been. Now several gray sharks ranging from three to six feet were darting around, chasing fish.

"We should probably head for shore now," Scott said, keeping a calm voice. "They're feeding and I'm getting tired." He didn't want to scare Laura.

"Okay." Laura looked at Scott. "Let's go."

They turned together and started paddling. *We're out further than I thought,* Scott realized. The boats where small on the horizon, probably a good half-football field away.

Scott felt his foot stinging. He kicked harder. He didn't want the sharks to smell the blood, because they were already feeding. He hoped they were too far to smell him for a while.

Scott glanced behind him in the water, He could see several gray reef sharks rising from the blue and darting into the coral. Scott looked ahead in the water. It seemed that the blue water had emptied of fish. Ahead, Scott made out dim shadows. *Just little ones,* he consoled himself. They swam from his right all the way to his left side until he had to glance sideways to see them. They were circling in closer behind him.

Laura was swimming extra hard and Scott noticed that he was starting to get tired. They must have been fighting an outgoing tide. The swim out here had been easy in comparison. Suddenly, the sharks seemed to spook and darted away into the blue. *Good, they left,* Scott thought. But just a moment later his relieved feeling was replaced with increasing anxiety. Two much larger sharks appeared, this time a little closer. Laura was scared, Scott could tell. She pulled him to the surface.

"What's going on?"

"Stay calm," Scott said, fighting the panic churning inside him. "I think my foot is bleeding, and they smell the blood."

The color drained from Laura's face. "What do we do?"

Scott's voice became firm. "Swim ahead of me, Laura. They smell me, not you." Scott coughed salty water.

"No," Laura said defiantly. "I'm staying with you."

The sharks were circling closer now. Scott forcefully reached out and pushed Laura with all his strength.

"Go." He forced his fiercest voice. "I'll be right behind you."

She looked at him helplessly, realizing she had no choice. She swam ahead of him, a fin darting past her side.

Scott swam for all he was worth, and then it happened again: almost instantly, the sharks disappeared. This time Scott didn't see anything but blue for almost a minute, and when he finally did see a shape, he knew instantly. A huge tiger shark, bigger then the ones Scott was used to seeing in the Marshall Islands, swam in a slow methodical circle around him. It was probably close to 12 feet long. Several other smaller sharks were swimming at a respectful distance behind him.

Scott continued swimming. He had lost sight of Laura, but he knew she was ahead of him. He watched the shark. It was obviously in hunting mode, swimming ever closer to him. He turned on his back and kicked toward shore as the shark swam behind him. He didn't want to take his eyes from it.

The shark was very interested. As soon as Scott started swimming away, it swam closer, hardly more then seven feet away in the water. Its eyes were cold and hungry.

Suddenly, it lunged toward Scott. Scott felt the icy fingers of fear and horror grip him. But right before he was sure the shark would bite him, it turned away with a quick twist of its head. Then it came back. This time, it was coming for Scott's foot, guided by his nose. It seized Scott's blue rubber flipper and tugged on it. Scott felt himself being jerked by the beast. He wildly kicked the shark with his free foot. His head and snorkel were jerked under water, and he inhaled a mouthful of salty water. Suddenly the flipper tore and the shark turned, flipper still in its mouth, attempting to swallow it. It was clear that the shark's bite had barely missed his toes.

The shark backed away, not liking being kicked in the head. It hadn't gotten any meat either, but it hadn't lost interest. It turned and circled again and a couple of other sharks were swimming closer.

Scott didn't notice the screaming engine until it was almost on top of him. The wake rolled him sideways and the shark darted under the boat. Hands were grabbing him and lifting him, dragging him into the boat. Scott flopped onto the floor, choking. Excited tourists surrounded him. Laura was crying in the front of the boat.

"You okay man? We would have never known if your girlfriend hadn't screamed so loud." The guide was patting Scott excitedly. The was the guy from the Paradise Snorkeling boat! Scott felt so relieved, he wasn't even embarrassed.

"He didn't get me, just my fin." Scott rolled onto his back.

The guide was pointing over the water. "We saw his fin coming toward you."

Scott staggered up and looked over the side. The water was completely empty now, just blue, and rising and falling in gentle swells, without a fin in sight.

"You shouldn't swim out this far without a boat," the guide said. "There's too strong of a current and the sharks are big out here."

"I know that now." Scott sat down on a bench and looked shakily to Laura. "Thanks." He looked at Laura with wordless gratitude.

"I'm just glad you're okay," she half-sobbed. "How horrible would that have been?" She gave a little coughing laugh in the middle of her sob.

Scott lowered his head and leaned on the wooden bow. The guide clambered up to him with a towel.

"We were just loading up to head back. You're very fortunate. I think the 'Man upstairs' was looking out for you, if you know what I mean." The guide's thick accent was excited. "A minute later or earlier, we wouldn't have been here."

Back at the beach, Scott profusely thanked the snorkel guide and staggered off the boat onto the sand, Laura helping him. As soon as the boat had driven away, and his feet were on solid ground, Scott sank to the sand, knees buckling underneath him.

Laura sat down next to him and they sat in silence, their minds registering the shock of what had just happened. Then Scott began to laugh, a strange fluttery laugh. He shook his head and lowered it into his hands.

"It's like I'm a magnet for catastrophe." A tear ran down his cheek and he still laughed. "I'm so glad to be alive." Laura rubbed Scott's back. she was laughing too. "I'm starving." Scott gripped the ground shakily. "I feel suddenly like I haven't eaten for a week."

"Wait right here, I'll get the picnic basket." Laura jumped up and sprinted up the beach. She returned from their hiding spot carrying the cooler and her bag. She plopped down next to him. "Here it is." She popped the lid open and a second later they where unwrapping their lunch of turkey sandwiches, potato salad and apple juice.

Scott paused from biting into his sandwich. "Oh darn, that shark ruined my flipper, and it was my uncle's."

"We can get a new one." Laura unwrapped her turkey sandwich,

Scott nodded. "It's not that, it's that John told me to be careful. Now I'll have to explain to him why the right flipper looks more like a shoe." He stopped to drink some apple juice. "I guess I deserve it though. I was pretty arrogant, I thought I knew better."

Laura was looking at Scott's foot. "Let me clean up that foot. I'm a nurse. I'll make sure it doesn't get re-infected." She leaned over and touched Scott's heel.

She had a little first aid kit in her bag. A few minutes later, Laura finished bandaging and cleaning Scott's heel.

"It's only one o-clock. Why don't we head up to the memorial and find a place in the shade where we can talk?" Laura suggested.

Up by the memorial, there was a green, grassy knoll overlooking the beach and several tall green trees grew, providing shade. Scott leaned comfortably against a grassy bank while Laura flopped down on the grass, chewing a piece of grass.

"So did you talk to John about Matthew last night?" Laura twisted the grass between her fingers.

"Didn't have a chance." Scott gazed affectionately at Laura. "I spent all my time getting ready for this snorkeling trip." He looked away and gazed over the water. "I will soon, though." The breeze rustled Scott's red hair. He glanced at Laura.

She was looking back at him. "What are the chances of us sitting together on the plane, and then meeting again together out here?" She shook her head. "We were total strangers four days ago, you know."

Scott was looking back over the ocean. "You wouldn't know it now, though." His voice held just a little wistfulness.

"I feel real good with you." He let out a breath of air. "Thanks for saving me from that shark." His voice sounded strange, almost awkward.

"All I did was swim for all I was worth." Laura was staring at the ocean. "When I realized you weren't right behind me, I didn't know what to do, then I saw a boat in front of me. I screamed, I really didn't do much."

Scott lifted his foot and held his shoe in his hand. "I know God was looking out for me. I should have died several times over this last few months." He set his foot down. "I've been struggling with whether I can really trust God." Scott laughed bitterly. "How stupid can I be?"

Laura sat up, eyes twinkling. "I hate to quote you, but wasn't it you who told me that God has the three legs of trust for us more than anyone?"

He nodded. "I think I'm just now beginning to realize it on a heart level." He looked away over the ocean. "I was really angry at God when I had to leave the Marshall Islands, I didn't trust him. I thought he was taking me away from everything good." He was quiet for a minute. "I don't know exactly why he did, but I've accepted it now, and I know God's looking out for me." He turned to Laura suddenly. "What do you think of mission work?" His eyes were deep and dreamy.

"Well, I, uh, don't know." Laura sat back. "I'm a nurse and I know I could help, but I've never been on more than a short trip away from the States." She looked back at Scott. "Why?"

"Oh, nothing." Scott's face flushed slightly, he looked away.

"No tell me," Laura coaxed. "There has to be a reason."

Scott looked away sheepishly. "I was just thinking about the airplane, and how I met you, and, and…" He was turning red.

Laura looked at him, her big eyes curious and just a little guarded. "Uh huh."

"Oh, I guess, I've just been enjoying spending time with you so..." Scott didn't finish his sentence for a second. "So I might like to get to know you a little better," he finished. He glanced at her quickly. She was smiling. She brushed a strand of hair from her forehead.

"I don't meet guys like you every day either. Maybe it would be good to get to know you a little better." She lifted her eyebrows. "So what are you saying?"

"Well, maybe we could go on a couple of dates." He looked at Laura. She was looking back. "What have the last days been?"

Scott looked taken aback. "I'm not sure," he admitted honestly. "I—don't know."

"There is one thing you should know about me, before we go any farther." Laura looked a little guarded. "The thing is...I have a son."

Scott gasped. "A son?" He felt like the air had just been let out of his lungs. "I didn't know that." He looked at Laura. She was looking at the ocean, but Scott saw the twinge of some expression he hadn't seen before on her face.

"I won't date a guy unless he accepts my son, first." She sounded like she was repeating a memorized speech. "If it wasn't for that, I would probably have been married by now." She sighed and looked at Scott. "I've met a lot of guys but none have been willing... " Her voice trailed off. "I guess I don't blame them. Not every man is willing to take on an eight-year-old."

"Where is he?" Scott asked hesitantly. It was the only thing he could think to say.

"He's with his dad in Idaho right now." She was looking at him again. "His name's Robert. He's my favorite little guy."

"Well, I'm not sure," Scott found himself struggling for words, he couldn't imagine adopting a boy when he was only 21.

"Let me make it easy for both of us." Laura again sounded like she was saying a rehearsed speech. "Let's just stay friends unless you are willing to take on that responsibility. If you consider it, and think it's an option, let's talk about it." She paused. "It's a big decision, so I don't expect you to make any decision without thinking it over." She leaned over and took Scott's hand in a handshake. "So just friends for now, and I don't have any hard feelings."

Scott nodded numbly. "Okay."

She leaned back against the bank, "I was looking for a opportunity to talk to you about it. I didn't want to scare you or anything, but I didn't want to give you the wrong impression." She plucked a piece of grass. "I'm sorry if I misled you."

"No, you did good." Scott sat up. "I respect you for that. I think you've had the three legs of trust for both me and your son Robert strongly." He sat in silence. "I just need to think about it." He felt disappointed.

Laura tossed pebbles in the grass. "Don't be glum, chum." She hit him with a small pebble, which bounced off his shirt. "I'm still your friend, and we got a lot we can do today." She looked serious. "I'm still really glad I met you, even if we never date. I learned a lot from you and I care about you like a brother."

Chapter 10

The ride back was awkward. Scott tried to avoid eye contact with Laura and wished desperately that the ride to the airbase would go faster. The white elephant in the car made the fun, easy conversation that had been normal before, difficult.

Even Laura's laughter and her jokes seemed a little forced and unnatural. Scott wiped his sweaty palms on his pants, finally at the gate.

"Can I see your ID?" The guard peered in the car. He glanced at the Air Force Chaplain sticker under the windshield and waved them through.

"Do I look like a chaplain to you?" The question seemed stupid once Scott heard himself ask it, but it was better than the heavy silence.

"Uh maybe." Laura looked up. "Hair's a little wild though, not distinguished enough." She gave a short laugh then was quiet.

A minute later, Scott arrived at Charles's house. He said goodbye to Laura as she got out of the truck. Neither said anything about 'next time' either. Scott felt miserable as he drove away. He slammed the steering wheel in his hand. How stupid could he be? How dumb of him to start liking some lady he met right off the bat, and with a kid!

"I must seem like a real jerk to her," Scott muttered to himself. Then he got back to the house. "Good." He sighed audibly. John and Ruth weren't home, and he definitely didn't feel like talking to anyone right now. Scott parked the truck and went into the house. He flung himself down on the couch, and pulled a pillow over his head with a tired, frustrated moan. "God," he said aloud. "I just about got eaten by a shark — I'm exhausted from that. And as if that weren't enough, I basically just ended my relationship with Laura, all because of a kid!"

Scott sat up and hurled the pillow across the room. It made a small poof sound as it landed on the other couch. The room stared back at him silently. "Aww, forget it!" He muttered. He sagged back down onto the couch and nestled his head into a cushion. "Got some more lighting to hit me with, God?" he moaned, "I must not be getting whatever you're trying to show me, so why don't you just tell me?"

He relaxed on the couch, totally spent, but just as his tired eyelids began to sag, Scott felt a strange peace envelope him. It seemed like a small voice whispered in his head, "I love you, and everything will be okay." Scott felt the muscles in his face relax as the peacefulness lulled him into an exhausted slumber.

Scott's eyes where still closed, but his mind suddenly jumped from the dream he was in. What was that? Keys jiggling in a lock. The sound of a door opening. Scott remained still on the soft cushions. He heard heavy steps. It must be his Uncle John. Scott's eyes fluttered open and he sat up, rubbing his cheek where it had pressed against the couch.

"Sorry, I didn't mean to wake you up!" Uncle John grinned at Scott, pausing at the edge of the couch. "Tired out from your dip in the ocean?"

Scott groaned. "You don't even know the half of it."

"Oh really?" uncle John sat down on the couch across from Scott, "How'd it go?"

Scott acted as if he hadn't heard. He sat rubbing his eyes. "Where's Aunt Ruth?" he asked sleepily.

"Oh she's at the church helping to decorate for a program." John leaned back, "I got off early because today's Friday, so that's why I'm home."

"Oh." Scott looked at John.

"So how was the snorkeling?" John asked again.

"I ruined one of your flippers. I need to replace it."

"Don't worry about it, Scott." John reached out and thumped Scott on the shoulder. "I have extras. I don't care about the flippers. I want to know if you had fun."

"Well, the flipper has something to do with that." Scott tapped his foot. "A tiger shark tore it while it was on my foot, actually."

John gave a little gasp. "Where? What happened?"

Scott related the tale of the swim with Laura and how he had gone out too far. "I'm sorry for being arrogant this morning. I think that happened because I was too cocky," he finished.

John sat on the couch, listening. "I'm glad you're all right. I'm also real proud of you for sending Laura ahead like that. You definitely demonstrated trust there." He paused. "I'll go diving with you any day, Scott."

"I'm a little shaken up." He admitted. "I wouldn't want to swim out there again right away."

John walked to the kitchen bar, loosening his tie and collar as he went. He ran a hand over his head in an attempt to smooth his hair. "There's nothing like getting back on a horse when it's bucked you off."

Scott had to laugh at that one, "Sure."

"Sounds like Laura handled the shark incident pretty well," John observed.

Scott was silent. Then blurted, "Did you know Laura has a son from her previous marriage?"

"No, I didn't." John was folding his tie now. "How'd that come up?"

Scott explained the conversation and how he had begun to like Laura. He felt terrible. "She's a real nice girl, but I don't know if I'm ready for a relationship. I'm definitely not ready for a kid." He bit his nail and looked up at John.

John was leaning quietly on the bar, listening. "This may not be what you were expecting me to say, Scott, but I know there's a girl out there for you somewhere. I don't understand everything that is going on in your life right now, but I know God has a plan for you and he's opening the doors." John looked thoughtful. "Keep the three legs of trust and you'll be a blessed person, and you'll have a good, happy marriage. I don't know why this happened, but God has a purpose."

Scott nodded soberly. "Thanks, John."

When Ruth arrived home, Scott had to retell the shark incident and also answer several questions about Laura. Ruth seemed genuinely concerned, and said she would call Charles to make sure Laura was feeling okay from the shark incident. "You don't have to worry about anything, Scott," she said. "I'll take care of all the girl stuff."

That evening after a delicious dinner, Scott excused himself to his room to think. After a while, he pulled out the green journal and leafed through it, pondering what it said. After a couple of minutes, he closed it with a thump and slid out of bed. He needed to talk to his uncle. He had to know. Did John think Matthew was really murdered?

Down the hall, he saw a light shining from under the door in his uncle's study. He walked softly down the hall and knocked. The door nudged open at the touch, and Scott saw John sitting in a black padded chair, reading a letter. John set it down and motioned for Scott to come in.

"How are you doing?" John asked, removing his reading glasses.

Scott held up the green journal in one hand. "I have some questions."

John looked from the book to Scott, then back. "Have you read the whole thing?" he asked.

Scott nodded. "Yesterday actually."

John leaned back in his chair and took an apprehensive breath. "Before we talk about anything, I want to tell you this. I wanted you to read that for two reasons, Scott. One, so you could understand the three legs of trust, and I thought reading it in Matthew's words would have a greater effect on you than if I just told you." John paused and cleared his throat. "The second reason I struggled though, is that I wasn't sure you could handle it." John looked at Scott. "I thought it was in your best interest to see what your uncle had written about the last days of his life." He scratched the back of his head. "I prayed about it seriously, and I only gave you the journal because I felt a peace about it, and I felt very compelled that you needed to read it."

Scott stood unsure. "Do you really think that there was foul play involved?" he stammered. "I mean, it's like he's going to confront Owen, and then the next day he dies."

John stood slowly from his chair. "Scott, all we know is what we read. I didn't have the opportunity to read this journal until five years after Matthew's death. It was in a box of things I found in Matthew's truck after the accident."

John picked up the green journal and turned it over. "Your Aunt Tiffany was in such grief that she couldn't handle dealing with any of Matthew's things then. I offered to rent a storage unit for my brother's personal belongings until she was able to go through them." He set the book on the table. "Two months later, Ruth and I received my assignment to be a chaplain here in Guam.

"Now just a couple of months ago, we went on leave back to Alaska. The storage unit had never been opened, and Tiffany told me that I could have or get rid of Matthew's things because it was too painful for her." John paused. "When I was in Alaska, it seemed like there was a lot going on under the surface. Things seemed very artificial between us and your family. All I'm saying is it seemed like they didn't want us too close, because they didn't want us to know something. But anyway, I decided to go through Matthew's things since no one else would. I found this journal." John reached down to the table and touched the book. "I brought it back with me to read. I felt strangely drawn to it for some reason. I left almost everything else in the storage unit." He stopped and turned to Scott. "I just finished reading Matthew's journal about a week before you arrived here, so it's new to me, too. Do not assume anything when you get back to Alaska." John shook his head. "Just be aware of the people you're dealing with, and how much you can trust them, and I would say to be careful with what you say around Owen.

Scott nodded. "You know the pastor that Matthew talked about in his journal? Tim?"

John looked up. "Yes, I do. He's the one who encouraged me to become a chaplain."

"Well I know him," Scott sat on a chair, "I'm going to call him tomorrow and let him know I'm coming home." He looked up at his uncle. "You know, he's the reason I came to the Marshall Islands. He was the one who helped me get in contact with the mission out there."

"I think that's a really good idea for you to get in contact with him." John nodded enthusiastically. "I think he's a very level-headed guy who'd be good for you to work with."

"I think he won't be happy that I'm coming back, though" Scott shook his head. "The reason I came out here to the islands was so that I could get away from the influences that hindered my growth at home. Subconsciously,

I couldn't break away from some of the things that were holding me back there, so I needed to leave. Tim really influenced that." He raked his hand through his hair. "And you're right. Something is going on between Tiffany and Owen. Mom told me that they were having some major difficulties in their marriage."

John nodded. "I knew there was something going on, even though I didn't know what. Scott, I want you to hear what I'm saying. Tread lightly and don't rock the boat when you get back. You do not want to make any inflammatory statements, and that's for your own good and also your family's. I would not trust Owen. You understand me?"

Scott nodded, "I understand."

*****

The next Saturday morning, after breakfast with his uncle and aunt, Scott asked if he could use the phone to make some calls.

"Go right ahead," John said. "But Ruth and I are going to a program at our church this morning, and you're invited to come if you'd like."

"Does Laura, I mean Charles, go to the same church as you?" Scott asked.

John nodded. "Yes."

"I think I'll just stay home then, and call back to Alaska, and relax." Scott pulled at his gray sweatpants, "I don't really feel like being around Laura right now."

John nodded. "That's fine, Ruth and I often invite people home for lunch so just be aware. We'll probably be back here around one."

Ruth walked into the room, heels clicking. She smelled of hairspray and perfume. "Can you do me a big favor Scott? There's a casserole in the oven on 350, and it should be done by 12:15. Could you take it out of the oven for me, since you're staying?" Ruth was now readjusting her hair in the mirror by the door. "I'd appreciate it, so we don't have to hurry home as soon as the program lets out."

Scott glanced at the clock. Only nine-thirty. "Sure, I can do that."

A minute later, John and Ruth bustled out the door, John busily tying his tie, while Ruth was talking to him about the program at church. "And we have to set up the microphone before..." The door closed behind them, a little wave of tropical air swooshing through the house.

"Ahh." Scott sat down on the couch and sighed. Finally peace. He could still faintly smell his aunt's hairspray as it settled in the air. "So I need to call home." He tapped his hand on the couch cushion, mentally preparing himself. He started to rise, but then sat back down. Alaska was a much different time zone, and his parents liked to sleep in on Saturdays. It was better to wait a little while. "I sure wish I knew what the time there is." He settled back in the couch. "Oh well." A soft beam of sunshine shone through the window and splattered lazily across the couch. It was pleasantly cool inside, and the warm sun felt good. *This couch makes me sleepy.* He sat back heavily. *I guess I'll just rest for a minute*, he thought drowsily. A minute later he was asleep.

Scott dreamed that a forklift was backing up toward him and its beeping was getting louder as it neared. The exhaust smelled smoky and a little bit like casserole... Casserole! Scott was instantly awake. He turned on the couch and stared blurrily into the kitchen. The smoke detector above the oven was beeping and a haze of blue smoke rose from the sides of the oven.

"Shoot," Scott muttered. He rolled off the couch, pillows landing on the floor with him. "Aunt Ruth's casserole." Scott staggered around the side of the couch. He reached the stove a second later and frantically jerked at the smoke detector. It popped loose from its place in the ceiling, now hanging from its wires, still beeping. "I got to get a chair so I can get the battery out of the stupid thing." Scott muttered. He was dragging a stool from the bar when Scott realized the oven was still on. He left the stool in the middle of the kitchen and began to frantically flip the dials on the stove. Hot smoke curled up around Scott.

"I have an enchilada casserole in the oven. It's one of John's favorites. My mother used to make the same recipe every Saturday..." Ruth was cut off mid-sentence as she opened the door. She stood starring at a scene she had not expected.

Scott was still in his gray sweat pants and orange T-shirt from breakfast. He dragged a stool across the kitchen floor, smoke around him, almost hitting his head on the smoke detector, which now hung precariously from the ceiling. His hair was pancaked sideways, flat on one side from where he had slept, and bushy on the other. He was now frantically flipping dials on the stove.

"What in the world?" John was halfway across the floor to the kitchen when he tripped over one of the couch cushions that had fallen to the floor. He fell, catching himself on the back of the couch with a sudden skidding slide. He was up and into the kitchen two seconds later.

Ruth, and her guests stood in the door, mouths agape, frozen for a second, then Ruth was skittering across the floor in her heels, and Charles hurried to help John carry the smoking casserole outside.

Laura hid a sudden urge to laugh in a discrete cough. She stood by her sister-in-law while the hubbub subsided.

"I'm so sorry," Scott was saying. He looked mortified. "I fell asleep on the couch, and overslept! I didn't realize how much time had gone by..."

John stood for a second, still holding the oven mitts. Suddenly he threw back his head and gave out a loud belly laugh. "I've always told Ruth that couch was a death sentence for studying. I swear, I sleep better on that couch than I do my own bed."

Everyone was silent for a second. Laura coughed once, then everyone was laughing. John leaned against the bar for support. He threw his arm affably around Scott.

"Don't worry about it, Scott, we'll throw together some hamburgers for lunch."

Ruth was laughing and she hugged Scott.

"I'll just excuse myself so I can get better clothes on," Scott said sheepishly. He retreated into the hall, with everyone still laughing.

"Come on into the kitchen, Grace, I'll need some help," Ruth said, still laughing.

Scott caught Laura's eye for one second, then looked quickly away, as he turned and hurried down the hall. It had twinkled ever so slightly, but probably because she was laughing at him, he figured. He closed the door behind him, and stood leaning on the door. "What do I do now?" He cupped his face in his hands. "Arrrh."

A knock sounded at the door a minute later. Scott was still leaning against the door. He stepped back to allow his uncle to enter.

"Scott, don't feel bad. It really is okay." John patted Scott on the shoulder. "I know you didn't mean to. It was a mistake."

"I know, I know." Scott put his face in his hands. "It's just Laura's here and everything." He stopped. "I'm sorry, John, I didn't mean to complain."

John patted Scott again. "Change and come out so you can be with everyone." He disappeared out the door.

*****

During dinner, everyone was talking, and Scott and Laura were sitting on roughly opposite ends of the table. He had planned it that way, making sure to sit down after Laura. John and Charles kept up a lively conversation, telling stories about awkward situations that kept everyone laughing. Scott was glad that he didn't have to say much, and he knew his uncle was telling stories to make him feel better.

He breathed a sigh of relief. He was feeling better, and the burgers really were good.

"Please pass the iced tea." Laura smiled sweetly at Scott from across the table.

He reached out, gripping the pitcher, looked blankly at Laura, then with a shove of his arm, he sent the pitcher sliding across the smooth table. Scott hadn't meant to shove it so hard. Laura reached out to try to stop it, but she was too late. The pitcher hit Laura's plate with a clunk and ice cubes and tea splashed and gurgled all over Laura. She gasped as the cold liquid hit her, reaching out and catching the pitcher in both hands.

Ruth was up instantly, wiping Laura with a napkin, while Scott apologized, feeling the blood burn in his cheeks.

"Looks like today isn't your day, Scott." Grace tried to loosen things up. "That's not so bad though, I remember a time I accidentally spilled a whole pitcher of punch on Charles when we were driving to church."

Everyone gasped. Charles threw back his head with a dry laugh,

"Oh yes, I was wearing my favorite Wemble tie, too. It wasn't the color of the punch." He winked at Scott. "Along with running late, and being the platform chairman, it made for quite an ordeal."

Everyone laughed. That is, everyone besides Scott. He was too embarrassed to manage more then a feeble cough...

Chapter 11

The phone rang, seeming to lag and echo.

"Hello, Ebi Mission. Can I help you?" said a native teacher Scott recognized.

"Hi, this is Scott. Is there any way I could talk with Jerry?"

The person on the other end paused. "Oh, hi Scott. I'll tell you what. If you can call back in fifteen minutes, I'll see if I can find him for you, okay?"

"Okay, I'll call back." Scott hung up the phone and sat heavily on a stool. He knew the drill there on Ebi. There was only one phone at the mission. It often took a long wait or an appointment reach any of the staff.

Scott sat back. He felt relieved now. Charles, Grace and Laura had all left, and after the late lunch, his aunt and uncle were now taking a nap. Scott waited for 15 minutes, then picked up the phone and dialed the Marshall Islands country code, then the number. After a few seconds, it began to ring.

"Hello, Ebi Mission. Can I help you?" the same native answered again.

"Yes. This is Scott. Did you find Jerry?"

"He's right here waiting, here he is."

Scott heard the phone being handed away.

"Hey Scott, how you doing?" Jerry's familiar voice drew Scott back to the islands.

He blinked and held the phone to his ear. "I'm doing all right."

"Well, if you had called any later, you would have missed me. Abra and us guys were just getting ready to go out in his boat when they found me."

Scott smiled at the memory. The Saturday afternoon boat rides, and evening worship on the beach with coconut husk fires.

"How's your foot healing up?" Jerry's voice brought Scott back to the moment.

"Oh great, it's healing great. No infection, and if I'm careful I won't need to even wear a bandage in a couple of days." Scott decided not to tell Jerry about how he had reopened it. Not yet, at least.

"We miss you here, Scott." Jerry sounded sincere. "It's not the same without you, especially for me."

"I know." Scott gulped, "I don't know why God had me leave yet, but I know there's a reason. I'll never forget the memories I have from there, though."

"That sounds like quite an attitude change," Jerry observed. "You were pretty upset when you left."

Scott adjusted the phone. "I still am sad, but there's nothing I can change by being angry with God, I just have to accept what happened and go forward. I know God had my best interest in mind, looking back now, even if I didn't believe it then."

"Hmm," Jerry said. "I've never heard you talk like that."

Scott shifted uneasily. "I haven't told anyone this before Jerry." He paused. "I had a dream when I was in the hospital, and it made quite an impact on me."

"When you where delirious and they gave you the anti-biotic?" Jerry asked.

"Yes. I'm pretty sure it must have been some time then, though I don't know exactly. That whole time is pretty fuzzy to me."

"You sure were carrying on a racket a few times. You kept the nurse and me busy, kicking your blankets off."

"Well, this is what I dreamed." Scott related the dream of the two roads and the tall teacher who he was sure was Satan. "Ever since that dream, I know God has a direction for me, and that this all happened for a reason."

The friends talked for several more minutes about how the mission was doing, Scott going to the doctor, and about Laura.

"I think she must hate me," Scott finished. "It's so weird."

"That's amazing," Jerry said. "I mean, you met her on the plane and everything."

Scott lifted his eyebrows as he talked. "And it wasn't like I was emotionally ready to meet her then, if you can imagine." He laughed, "I'm amazed that I didn't freak her out on the airplane."

The two friends reminisced, stalling the goodbye they both knew would come. Scott cleared his throat. "I'm getting ready to go back home to Alaska now, Jerry. I'm going to call my parents to get my tickets after I hang up with you." He paused. "I'm a little apprehensive." After a few more minutes of talking, Scott said goodbye. "Good to talk to you, Jerry, I'm really thankful for all you did for me."…

After he hung up on Jerry, Scott pulled on the phone cord a couple of times. He knew he was procrastinating making the call home. He felt like it was the same with Alaska and his parents, no matter how far he managed to get away from home. Whether it was the tropics or a different state, something seemed to always draw him back: an accident, a connection, something. It was like he was on a massive cord, and no matter how far he'd run to escape, he'd always be pulled back to confront what he was running from.

With a deep breath, he lifted the receiver and dialed the number. As usual, his dad answered.

"Hello?" He sounded like he had just woke up.

"Uh, hi, Dad. This is Scott."

"Oh. Hi." His dad's voice was brisk. "What's up?"

"I'm doing quite a bit better, Dad. I think I'm ready to fly back now."

"Oh, really?" his dad sounded a little annoyed and surprised. "Didn't you just get there two days ago?"

Scott took a breath. "No, Dad, I've been here almost a week now."

"Oh, I must have lost track of time." His dad sounded like he was writing something, "Call me back in two hours, and I'll tell you when to go to the airport. I just need to call the airlines. I'm assuming you want me to buy the ticket?"

Scott felt his face flush. "I can pay you when I get back, Dad. I'll—"

"Forget it, Scott. Don't make promises you can't keep." His dad's voice was cutting.

"I will, Dad, I made the money to come out here—"

"Just call back in two hours." The line went dead.

Scott heaved a breath and banged the receiver down. His dad always made him feel so small and worthless. He had the money! He turned as he heard a noise.

"Everything okay, Scott?" John stood in the hall behind him, a look of concern on his face.

"Oh yeah. My dad's making my tickets home now." Scott began to turn away, dejected.

"What is it? I think I'll understand." John walked out of the hall and put a hand on Scott's shoulder. "I really do think I might."

Scott hesitated, then turned back, frustration in his face. "I just can't understand what my dad's problem is. He always puts me down." He reached into his back pocket and pulled his wallet out. "Here, let me give you some money for letting me stay here." He began to pull a wad of 20s from its folds.

"Stop, Scott, don't be ridiculous." John held both hands up. "I won't take any of your money. I'm glad you came.

Save that money so you can come back again." John shook his head. "Now, you just stick that back in your pocket and don't let me see it again."

Scott replaced his wallet in his pocket at his uncle's prodding. "It's – It's just my dad just insulted me about not being able to pay for my ticket. I can't help it that the return money I had saved was used for sending me here." Scott sat down on the couch suddenly. "I don't know what to do. I'm dreading going home so much. I have so much there I just want to leave behind."

John sat on the couch across from Scott quietly. "This may sound weird, but I want to tell you something very important." He paused. "When I was your age, I followed my brother Matthew and left home. I couldn't stand it there. I hated my dad so much." He paused, eyes misting at the memory. "It was a hard time, but a certain man told me some advice that changed my life, and this is what he said." John's eyes were bright now as he explained. "I was telling him how much I hated my dad, and that I was running away from my problems, basically. He told me, 'John, embrace your pain, stop running from it, you'll be a better man for it.'"

John turned to Scott now. "You may be trying to escape from your past, but when you do that, it will always catch up with you and pull you down. I believe the reason you are going home is so that you can face your demons, and conquer them, so that you can embrace your weaknesses and make them into strengths." He looked at Scott with intensity. "Embrace them." He reached out a hand and took Scott's in a firm grip. "Scott, I love you for my brother's sake." His hand shook slightly. "I want you to come back and visit me, and when you do, I don't want it to be because you're running from something. I want it to be because you want to do some shark diving with me." His face suddenly split into a wide smile, "You hear what I'm saying?"

Scott nodded. The idea was strange. Embrace your pain? He didn't want to do that! "Why should I embrace my pain? Logically, I want to get as far from it as possible."

"Because it's the only way you can truly heal from it. If you hide it, it will resurface and sabotoge your life." John looked back at Scott evenly. "Trust someone who has had to learn that the hard way."

"Who told you that?" Scott cocked his head.

"Well, if you must know, it was a certain man I think you actually know." John smiled.

"It's not Pastor Tim, is it?" John nodded. Scott gave a shaky laugh. "It seems like something strange he'd say."

"He's a wise man, Scott." John had a serious expression on his face.

Scott looked down and away, and nodded, "I know. It's just I have a lot of pain to embrace then," he said huskily.

"It's worth it, Scott. When you embrace your pain, it allows those wounds to heal, and it makes you stronger."

Scott nodded. "Thanks, Uncle John. You've been really good to me. I want to come back and go shark diving with you, too."

Chapter 12

The 747's wheels bounced and rolled as the plane touched down onto the runway. Scott peered out the window at the short trees that raced by the edge of the tarmac. Anchorage, Alaska. His dad would be waiting. Scott breathed a heavy breath. He already felt a million years removed from the tropics, even though he had just been in Guam that night before. He remembered waving to his uncle and aunt and watching Ruth wipe a tear from her eye as he disappeared down the ramp. Would he ever see them again?

Scott felt the cool fall air rush into the plane as the door opened. "Currently 59 degrees," the stewardess had said. He shivered. He had grown accustomed to the 80-degree weather of the islands.

As Scott emerged from the plane he saw his dad, Robert Calloway, MD. He was standing tall and in a leather jacket, arms folded across his chest and a tie showing below the expensive leather.

"Hi, son." His dad stepped forward and caught Scott in a sideways hug. "Glad to see you." Scott shivered just a little bit. "Looks like the islands made you soft."

"I know." Scott looked down at his tanned legs sticking from his khaki shorts. "I forgot that the end of August was cool up here." He held his arm up next to his dad's. "See the sun difference.

His dad's white wrist and forearm contrasted heavily with Scott's tanned and freckled arm. His dad had to pull up his sleeve to compare.

"You'll probably get skin cancer," Robert grunted. "C'mon, let's get your bags."

The two headed to the baggage claim and waited with the crowd.

"So how was your stay at John's?" Robert asked.

"Oh, good. I spent a lot of time of with a girl I met there though, so I wasn't there a lot. They were really nice to me," Scott finished and looked up at his dad.

He nodded, expressionless. His thinning hair left a bald spot shining. "I just wondered if they were bothered." Little lines in Robert's face showed as he scowled. "Do I need to write them a check for your stay, Scott?"

Scott shook his head. "No, they said nothing of the kind. I didn't hardly cost them anything anyways. I tried to give them $100 when I left, but John refused, and told me to save it so I could come back and snorkel with him."

"And your hospital visit?" Robert watched Scott reach out and heave a bag from the carousel.

"Doctor didn't do anything other than just give me a cream for my foot. I would be surprised if it cost much, if anything at all." Scott set the suitcase down with a heave. "Let's go Dad, I have my bag." Scott didn't like how his dad treated him like he was so naïve.

"I'm still going to write them a check." Robert scowled. "I don't want them telling tales of us."

"They wouldn't tell any tales, Dad, I know them." Scott protested. "I had a lot of fun with them."

"A lot of fun, eh?" Robert shook his head. "You haven't lived as long as me, Scott, and if I know anything from my 12 years of college, it's that money is very important to people."

That ended that. Scott knew better than to argue with his dad about his college experience. He sat quietly in the front seat as his dad pulled out of the airport. Scott watched as the Ted Stevens International Airport sign went past his right side, rows of petunias and pansies planted around its base.

"There's already some fall colors in the trees," commented Scott, glancing at several tinges of yellow in the passing birches. "It's only August 21."

Robert nodded and grunted he pulled into a post office. "Better get that check mailed off." He pulled an envelope from the door and wrote out a check for $300.

Scott watched. In the memo, he wrote: *For distant relative inconvenience.* Scott turned and stared out the window, frustrated.

"You stand in line to mail this, Scott. I think that's fair since you're the reason for it." Robert reached across the seat and handed the preaddressed envelope and check to Scott. "Make sure to get it certified. I'll be waiting here in the truck."

Scott opened the door and stepped out of the truck, anger and frustration seething inside him.

"Do you have enough money to mail it?"

"Yes, Dad, it's not a problem." Scott closed the pickup door and walked into the post office. He knew better than to ask his dad for postage money.

An hour later, Scott and his dad were nearing Wasilla. They had talked about the economy and the newfangled Internet. Scott had told his dad some stories from the Marshall Islands. It was good to talk with his dad, despite his rude comments. He felt that his dad was genuinely glad to see him, as long as Scott kept him in a good frame of reference.

"So I suppose you're done messing around and are gonna get a job so you can go to school, then?"

"I'm not sure what I'm going to do yet, honestly, Dad," Scott replied. His face was pressed against the window. "The change is so sudden. I'm still trying to figure out what

I'm going to do now. I was expecting to be in the Marshall Islands for two more years."

"Well, you flaked out on that. Make sure you don't flake out on life."

At home, Scott greeted his mother. He thought she looked older than last time he'd seen her. *It must be the extra gray hair,* Scott mused.

"You're back just in time." She hugged him again. "You're like a board, Scott, loosen up."

"Oh, sorry," Scott mumbled. It wasn't that pleasant to have her squeezing him.

She was still holding on to him at arm's length as she talked. "We're having a family dinner tomorrow night so everyone can see you." She beamed at him. "Your Uncle Owen and Aunt Tiffany will be coming over, along with your brother, Phillip."

Scott stepped back, discreetly releasing himself from his mom's hold. "Since when has Owen been 'Uncle?'" He twitched his fingers like quotation marks.

"You better watch your mouth, Scott, before you find yourself in a bad spot," Robert warned menacingly. He had returned from the kitchen with a shot glass of whiskey between his fingers.

"I'm just asking," Scott protested.

"And I'm just telling you," Robert replied evenly. "Owen was best man at my wedding, and he's still my best friend. If you want to stay under my roof, in my house," Robert's voice rose in a crescendo, "you better not so much as look at him wrong. Are you picking up what I'm laying down?" He glanced darkly at Scott before draining the shot in a single gulp.

His mom glanced at Scott apologetically, wringing her hands. "Scott, why don't you take your suitcase up to your room and then bring me any dirty laundry you want washed."

"And bring a quarter, too, because laundry service isn't free around here anymore, either." Robert slammed his shot glass down on the counter and reached for the remote that sat by his favorite recliner. "Time for sports." He sighed and sank into his chair, shooting a sideways glance at Scott. "Don't keep your mom waiting."

Scott hurried upstairs. It felt like dark walls had sprung around him and he was being suffocated by the gloom. He felt a familiar vault door swing shut across his heart. His dad's words bore into his mind, and there was no opening that vault door now, he knew. No one in this house knew the combination, not even him. It had been over a year since he had felt this stony hardness. He hadn't needed it in the Marshall Islands. It had taken him a while to unlock this mysterious vault door over his heart, and now it had slammed back shut on him. He had developed this hardness as a child. It was normal back then. He had thought everyone must be this way. His dad telling him he was no good and yelling at him daily, while his older brother met with constant approval. Scott winced physically as he stepped into his room. Maybe his heart wasn't completely locked from the pain yet. This house with so many memories. He turned in the door to face his brother's room directly across the hall.

The door was open and the lights were on. It was neatly cleaned and rows of Star Wars figurines stood in perfect order across the dresser. A poster on the door read, "The Force is with you." Scott stepped across the hall and into the open door. A picture as large as a small poster was hanging above the figurines. It was of his brother, Phillip, in a cap and gown shaking a smiling Robert's hand. Gold letters boldly embossed a title across the bottom. Phillip Robert Calloway receiving a diploma for a bachelor of science in psychology.

The picture was arranged so the lamp shone directly onto it, giving it a prominent glow. Scott sighed and stepped back across the hall and into his own room. No such picture adorned his wall. His room was dark and dusty. A stack of boxes and some buckets blocked half the room.

He flipped the light on and discovered that two cats where sleeping on his bed while a cat box sat in the corner. Didn't his parents remember he was allergic to cats? Scott angrily shooed the fat cats from his bed and stifled a sneeze. He had to get the window open. He cranked it open and hurried into the hall for fresher air.

Downstairs, he met his mom in the laundry room with a small armload of clothes. "This is everything, Mom. I didn't bring much back." He laid the pile on the washer.

"I'm sorry about your father, dear." She looked flustered as she nudged the laundry room door and lowered her voice. "Your father is very easily angered when anyone says anything about Owen at all, since he loaned him that money." She shook her head. "Whenever I bring it up, he just gets angry and watches TV." She turned and glanced out the door discreetly. "I'm worried too, because he's been drinking a lot recently."

"I don't care, Mom. I don't want to get involved." Scott's voice was flat. "I'm just going to try to stay out of his way." He turned, frustrated. "Why is there a cat box in my room?"

"Oh, I'm sorry, our cat box used to be in here, but your dad moved it so he could have room for a new safe." She touched a large metal box as she spoke. "I couldn't talk him out of it."

Scott glanced at the polished silver safe curiously. "Why did he get that?"

She shook her head. "I don't know. Foolish, if you ask me, but he says he needs it for business purposes."

"I don't know why you'd need a safe for counseling and describing antidepressants, but I do know there's no way I can sleep in my room unless we get all that cat stuff out of there."

"I'll see if I can arrange something. Just let me deal with it. Your dad is in a bad mood right now."

"I could have guessed that," Scott grunted. "Is my truck still parked by the woodshed? I think I'll go for a drive."

Scott went out the garage door so he wouldn't have to walk past his dad. All he knew was that he needed to get out, before anything more happened. His old Chevy pickup fired up without any problem. His dad had used it for hauling firewood. Scott noticed that the fuel needle was right on empty, though he was sure he had left it with a full tank. Better not complain about that. His dad would be sure to turn it around on him.

Scott arrived at the gas station a few minutes later and stood outside while the fuel pump slowly chugged away. He stuck his hands in his pockets and turned so the wind could rustle his hair. The smell of diesel drifted up to him from the pump.

He paid the attendant, grabbed a Sprite, and pulled away from the station. He turned his truck toward Palmer and let one hand steer as he sipped his soda. He needed time to think. The familiar sights along the Palmer-Wasilla highway greeted his eyes as he drove: Wasilla Lake, a gravel pit, the fire station and potato farm. He looked up toward the large snow-capped Pioneer Peak rising majestically to his right. His gaze swept the valley, Matanuska Peak, Lazy Mountain; he'd climbed both of them before. *If I can find a new start, this isn't a bad place really,* he mused. Scott rolled down the window and let the cool fall air roll into the cab around him. It smelled of birch and grass.

Halfway to Palmer, Scott turned off the highway. A minute later he was rolling up at a familiar brown house. He switched the engine off and stepped out onto the soft gravel. A golden retriever barked from the porch and trotted with tail wagging to greet him. Scott stroked the silver muzzle.

"You still remember me, Wagner?" The golden retriever gave a friendly thump of his tail and turned his trusting eyes up to Scott. Scott patted the dog's head. "Of course you do, old boy." He turned and headed toward the door, the old dog walking next to him, brushing him with his furry tail.

Scott rang the old doorbell and waited. He heard soft footsteps and then the door opened. A silver-haired man with a bushy gray beard stood in the door, wearing round reading glasses and fur slippers. He held a sandwich in one hand.

"Scott?" The man swayed for a second. The half-eaten sandwich loosened in his hand and a piece of chicken fell to the floor. Quick as a flash, the old dog licked it from the porch, barking excitedly. "Scott, it is you! I sure wasn't expecting to see you in this half of the world." The tall man stepped forward and stooped slightly as he shook Scott's hand and caught him in a friendly hug. He stepped back, his blue eyes bugging slightly behind his glasses as he stared at Scott. "You caught me having a bite to eat. I wasn't expecting company for another half an hour, but come on in, lad, you're welcome to join me." He chuckled softly as he turned in the door.

"Tim, I'm so glad to see you." Scott stepped through the door. "I wasn't expecting to be here either."

Tim walked across the living room and sat down in a leather-backed chair. "Well, whatever happened?" He reached across the coffee table and took another chicken sandwich from a stack. "Care for one?" He held the plate out to Scott, who took a sandwich and bit hungrily into the soft white bread, mayonnaise and peppered chicken slices.

"Thanks. I'll explain." Scott stopped eating. He related to Tim his tale. "So now I'm here." He spread his hands. "I blew in with the fall breeze."

Tim sat facing him calmly, a leg drawn up across his lap, his slipper-clad foot tapping softly. Other than that, he seemed very relaxed. He took another bite of sandwich and paused to lick the mayonnaise off the tip of his finger.

"Well, sounds like an interesting story." He nodded. "What are you wanting to do now?" He peered at Scott, then he began to leaf through an open book next to him. He set it down a minute later.

"I don't know exactly," Scott admitted. "But I'd like to find a job and a place to stay other than my parents' house. I know that for sure."

Tim wiped his mouth with a napkin. "Your dad being hard to live with already?"

Scott shook his head dismissively. "I don't want to give him the chance."

He nodded. "Well, lets just take this one step at a time. Up until now, I was thinking you were on the other side of the ocean, teaching school, and diving with man-eaters." His eye held a twinkle. "At least you won't have to worry about sharks here."

He laughed at Tim's soft humor. "I guess that's right."

Tim looked thoughtful. He uncrossed his leg, and thumbed through an address book sitting by the chair. "I do know of one thing, though. I'll have to give a guy a call. Speaking of shark attacks, how do prosthetic limbs sound to you?"

Scott looked confused. "I'm not sure what you mean. I still have my foot."

Tim smiled knowingly. "I know a man who is in the business of making artificial limbs. He needs a steady assistant he'd be willing to train into his company, if he took a liking to him."

Scott leaned forward. "Making artificial legs?"

Tim nodded. "And feet. You'd be making pretty good money once you get going, too." He eyed Scott thoughtfully. "The man I'm talking about goes on trips to Cambodia twice a year. There are a lot of people who've had their feet blown off by land mines there." He turned and looked out the window. "I just talked to him, and he was saying he needed a young guy to help him. It's the first thing that comes to mind, if you're looking for something different."

"Let me think about it, Tim. I have something else I need to talk to you about, too. It concerns Matthew and Owen, and a journal I read in Guam."

Tim looked at Scott quizzically. "Really? I'm very curious. I want to hear all about it." He glanced at his watch. "The problem is, I wasn't expecting you to be here and I have an appointment with a Methodist minister in five minutes."

"Oh," Scott said, disappointed. "When would be a good time?"

"Tomorrow night, I'll be free," Tim said. "I'm sorry that it can't be sooner. If I'd known, I would have had my schedule open for you."

Scott stood shakily from his chair. "Thanks, Tim, I really appreciate it. I want you to know that."

Tim smiled. "No problem." He heaved himself from his chair and headed to the kitchen, carrying his sandwich plate. He stopped by Wagner and let the dog lick the crumbs from it. "You and I go way back, and I'll make sure to have time for you. Eight o' clock sound good?"

"Yes, it sounds great, but we're having a family dinner tomorrow night, so I don't know if I can make it."

Tim nodded. "Then come over the next morning, and if you really need to talk, you can come a little after eight." He turned back into the kitchen.

"Okay, I'll see you." Scott waved and petted Wagner as he left. "Good boy."

As Scott got into his truck, a gray Corolla pulled up next to Scott with a distinguished looking man inside. He nodded gravely to Scott as he backed out of the driveway. It seemed that there was quite a demand for Tim these days. Scott shook his head. He turned his truck and headed for home.

Robert ignored Scott when he came inside. He was still slouched in his chair, watching a football game. He glanced over his shoulder. "Your mom's in your room." He turned back to the TV.

Scott walked up the stairs and found his mom finishing vacuuming the bed, the cat boxes had disappeared, but the cat smell still remained.

"Where's Phillip?" Scott asked.

"Oh he doesn't come home except for weekends. He's living in Anchorage and doing his apprenticeship with a doctor there." His mom was busily fluffing a pillow. "We keep his room neat so he has a place to stay if he ever decides to stay here. Didn't your dad tell you?"

Scott shook his head. "He told me he was apprenticing in Anchorage, but I didn't know he wasn't at home."

"Your father is so proud of him." Mom was plugging a fan in, "He would be proud of you, too, if you would just go to school and make our family look good."

Scott's face darkened. "Mom, I'm different from Dad. He and Phillip both love cats. I'm allergic to cats. They both are psychologists, I'm not interested in psychology. They agree on everything. Dad and I clash on everything. I just don't understand why you can't get that."

His mom looked a little upset. "I know your dad's not perfect, but I think he's right about you needing to go a different direction. Your Uncle Matthew, bless his heart, did you wrong when he directed you to mission work.

Scott was fuming. "He died before he ever did that. The only work he ever directed me toward was construction!"

"You know we never approved of you running off to the Marshall Islands and wasting a year of your life, and it looks like we were right. You're right back where you started."

Scott shook his head. "That's not true Mom, I don't regret it for a second."

She picked up the vacuum. "Well, I guess we differ on that. Anyway, I'm going to make dinner, come down and talk with your dad and me." She turned and walked out the door.

Scott sat on the bed. Every time he came into this house, he felt himself close up and angry feelings run around inside. He banged his pillow, then stifled a sneeze. It still smelled like cats!

*****

The next morning, Scott awoke to his dad knocking on his door. "Since you're just sleeping in and waiting for something to do, I left a list of things I'd like done on the table. I'm going to actually go to work now, so I'll see you tonight." He turned and walked out, leaving Scott sitting up in his bed, feeling stuffy and confused.

Where am I? He rubbed his eyes. It was 7:30 AM, and he had a stuffy nose and headache. The cats. It all flooded back to him. He was at home.

Downstairs, he found a list of items written on a neat Post-It note on the table: stack wood, move tires, take trash to dump, paint trim, and empty cat box. That was adding insult to injury!

Scott could hear the water running upstairs, so he knew his mom was still in the shower. He helped himself to some Cheerios and slipped into a coat and boots and headed outside. The stack of wood was enormous, so it took him until almost noon to finish it. He went on to the other items, only coming in for a quick lunch. The afternoon was passing quickly.

"Thanks for helping, Scott." His mom opened the screen door. "It's almost 4 o' clock, everyone's coming at 6, are you finishing up?"

"Yes, Mom." Scott turned, wiping the paintbrush across the roller pan. "I'll just take the trash to the dump then."

When Scott arrived back from the Matanuska Land Fill, two new cars were parked in the driveway, a shiny Porsche and his dad's pickup truck. Scott had to carefully steer his old truck around the new cars to get to his parking spot next to the woodshed.

Scott stepped from the cab, took a deep breath and headed for the front door. Inside, his brother Phillip was leaning against the counter, a glass of wine in one hand, his white shirt unbuttoned, a heavy gold chain showing below the collar.

"Hey brother." Phillip turned to Scott. "You back from the dump, I mean the islands?"

Scott's dad laughed from behind the counter. "I think you got them confused, Phillip."

Phillip leaned on the counter for a second, smirking at his own humor. He glanced at Scott, noticing his offended expression. "I'm totally joking." He stepped forward. "Give a brother a hug."

Scott stiffly hugged Phillip. "Good to see you." He looked out the window, changing the subject. "Whose Porsche is that outside?"

Philip turned from the counter. "You talking about that cherry looking car in the driveway?" He smiled. "It's mine, got it as a graduation present. You'll get one if you finish your degree, too." He turned back toward the living room, "She purrs like a kitten. The girls like that car, too." He winked at Scott and walked toward the living room. "When's Owen and Tiff getting here?"

"Should be soon." Mom made her first appearance, moving in from the hidden pantry, carrying some croutons and a block of cheese. "Scott, help me set the table, will you?"

Scott turned and walked to the kitchen, taking a stack of plates from his mom. His dad and Phillip were on the couch, arguing about who was going to win the Superbowl. Scott was quietly setting the silver dessert forks around the table when a Suburban rumbled up the driveway. Scott glanced up from the table, looking out to see the sign printed on the side of the vehicle. ***Davis Construction and Renovation.*** He shuddered, despite himself.

"Uncle Owen and Aunt Tiffany are here," Mom called to the living room. "Come be social."

His dad and brother rose and made their way into the kitchen just as Owen stepped through the screen door.

"Good to see you, man!" He pumped Phillip's hand. "And who've we got here?" He pointed and smiled at Scott. "Is this Limpfoot?" Everyone laughed.

"Hey, Owen." Scott stepped forward and shook his hand.

"Not much of a limp, though." Owen eyed Scott. "I was told right, wasn't I?"

"Yes, you were." Scott explained, "But my foot is healed, so you wouldn't know now."

"Well, you'll have to tell us all about your adventure." Aunt Tiff stepped into the circle. "Let me take my coat off and help you in there." She turned to where Scott's mom was still preparing a salad in the kitchen.

Soon everyone was sitting around the large oak table, fresh herbed salmon, salad and rolls arrayed out in front of them. Scott was used to saying a prayer before each meal, but his mom didn't wait, and was soon spooning salmon onto plates. "Pass the tartar sauce and lemons."

Phillip wiped his mouth with a napkin. "Good fish Mom."

Owen forked a pink slab onto his plate. "You catch this yourself, Robert?"

Robert shook his head. "One of my buddies went to Seward silver fishing this last weekend, caught his limit plus a king." He nodded. "Good silver run this year."

"We gotta go, some time." Owen nodded. "If things get under control in the business, we might be able to spare a weekend."

Robert nodded. "Tell me about it."

Scott looked up from his plate. He was about to ask about the business when his aunt spoke. "How's fishing out in those islands, the Martha Islands? Isn't that what they're called?"

"No, actually it's the Marshall Islands," Scott corrected. "The fishing out there is good, though it's a lot different from Alaska."

"Tell us about it." Scott's dad squeezed a lemon over his fish.

"Well, I did a lot of spear fishing, when I was there. Grouper, parrotfish, jack tuna and snapper." Scott was hesitant, not sure how much to say.

"How'd that go?" Owen was staring at Scott.

"Oh, good." Scott told how the natives sometimes fished with dynamite, and talked about how he used to fish off the pier for sharks. "The water's really beautiful there, great visibility and warm, lots of reefs and fish. It's a whole other world."

"Sounds like you got good fringe benefits 'working.'" Phillip used his fingers as quotation marks. "Is that all you did out there, Scott? Swim and fish?"

Scott gulped. "No, I taught school and worked quite a bit. We only had a couple days off a week. The rest of the time, I was working."

"Well, I guess I'll go somewhere tropical sometime," Phillip stated. "But I'll go when I can afford to play seven days a week." He smirked at Scott.

The dinner conversation continued, mostly talking about inconsequential subjects. Scott remained reserved, careful about his choice of words and subject matters. Though everyone seemed happy, there was a certain tension Scott detected, though he couldn't quite put his finger on what it was.

Maybe it was when Owen commented about how Tiffany needed to watch his mother, Jean, cook fish, because, "You can always learn from the experts." Tiffany looked up, eyes flashing, but she said nothing.

After dinner, the group moved to the living room. Scott's mom brought pie and ice cream, and Robert turned on the nightly news.

"I'll get some of my spiced rum, that will go good with dessert, won't it, Owen?" Robert grunted as he sat up from his chair. A minute later he returned with a glass bottle and several small glasses. He poured several glasses and handed them around.

Scott shook his head. "I don't want any."

"Still too good to drink?" Robert muttered.

Phillip looked at Scott as he sipped his glass. "Am I going to hell, Scott?" he asked sarcastically.

"No, I don't feel that way, the alcohol just doesn't agree with my stomach." Scott squirmed uneasily.

"Don't bother him," piped up Tiffany. She walked into the room carrying a piece of pie from the kitchen. "I don't want any rum either, and there's nothing wrong with that."

Owen grunted. His eyes glinted as he took a sip of his drink and leaned back. "There's nothing wrong with a drink, either."

Scott was afraid to drink with Owen. He had never been one to handle alcohol very well, and it always made him talk freely. He knew that if he loosened up too much, he might say something he wouldn't want to. He also remembered how his mom had told him months earlier that his dad and Owen were drinking a lot more than usual. At the time she had said it, Scott hadn't thought about it much. He had been too busy with life at the mission to worry about matters in distant Alaska, but now that he was here, it seemed much closer and relevant.

Scott looked around the living room. His dad and Owen were visibly relaxing as the alcohol flowed through them. His brother, Phillip, made witty remarks and sipped his glass, a smirk across his face. His mom and aunt were in the kitchen, talking. Scott was intrigued. Before he had left, he had never remembered his parents drinking with guests, or at all for that matter, other than the occasional glass of wine at a New Years party. This was strange for his dad. What had changed?

Scott decided to start a new conversation. "Why don't we all plan a fishing trip to Seward, Dad, before the summer's over? I haven't been there for a couple years now."

His dad turned in the couch. "Can't do it." He shook his head. "Don't got the equipment."

Scott cocked his head, confused. "What do you mean, we don't have the equipment? Don't we have Matthew's old fishing boat and gear?"

"Don't have the boat anymore." His dad shook his head.

Scott frowned. "Did you sell it, Dad?"

"It was actually my boat, Scott." Owen looked up from his chair darkly.

"Oh, okay, I didn't know that." Scott responded meekly. It had been parked at his dad's house after Matthew died though. He was confused.

"We went out deer hunting, Dad, Owen and I," Phillip piped up. "Long story short, the boat's still stranded out there on a gravel beach, engines both dead, and a hole in it."

Aunt Tiffany and Scott's Mom walked back into the room.

Owen stirred on the couch again. "The boat was a piece of trash from the beginning. I don't feel that bad about it." He poured himself another glass. "Matthew didn't know the first thing about boats. Just the first few times I took it out, it started acting up. I couldn't help that he passed a lemon on to me."

Scott remembered how his uncle had bought that boat. He had carefully poured over its manual, and talked to its previous owner for several hours before he had paid the hefty price, $12,500. Scott remembered how that boat had been his uncle's pride and joy. He had carefully cleaned and oiled it, had a new outboard motor installed. He had taken his family fishing in it several times before his death. It had never ever had trouble when his uncle used it. Scott had assumed it was his dad's after Matthew's death, but Owen must have claimed its ownership after he married Tiffany. He held deed to her deceased husband's property. Scott was sure his dad hadn't resisted Owen, even if he hadn't liked it. Scott already knew that it was Owen who had ruined the boat. That was obvious by his dad's silence.

"Matthew sure did pay a lot for that boat for it being a lemon, though," Scott couldn't help saying.

"Like I said he didn't know anything about boats," Owen said. "I think he must have been naïve and stupid to be swindled into paying as much as he did."

Scott's dad was still silent. Everyone sat mutely for a second. Aunt Tiffany cleared her throat. "When I was married to Matthew, he always took very good care of that boat. We never had any trouble with it at all. Why don't you just admit that it was you who ruined it?" Her tone was icy.

Owen sat up and slammed his empty glass down on the table angrily. "Since when were you a boat expert, Tiff?" His eyes were red. "I think I know a tad more about what I'm talking about than you. Why don't you keep your focus on learning to cook the fish?"

Tiff bristled. Everyone sat in stunned silence. "It's pretty hard for me to cook fish, since you destroyed the boat we caught them with, don't you think, Owen? Or do I not know what I'm talking about? Just like Matthew didn't know anything about boats?"

Owen was standing shakily, the vein showing red above his forehead. "Tiffany, you're as stupid as your old husband who fell off the roof." Saliva dripped from his intoxicated lips. "I can see why you two were so good together now," he snarled.

Robert stood. "Now, now, we're all family here, let's not get out of hand." He tried to stand between Tiff and the irate Owen, using his calm psychiatrist voice.

Tiffany shrugged him aside, like he wasn't there. "You pompous ass, Matthew never treated me as badly as you do!" She flung her napkin angrily at him, and turned. "I'm leaving." She marched sobbing toward the door.

"Not without me, you aren't, Tiff." Owen stumbled toward the door. "You wouldn't want something bad to happen to you, would you, Tiff?" His tone was threatening. Robert was trying to protest, but the larger Owen moved him aside. "Thanks for the purty," he slurred. "Sorry Tiff has a forked tongue like she does. I would have liked to stay longer." With that, the two stumbled out into the darkness, Tiffany crying and Owen talking loudly. "Just shurt up and get in the truck and drive, woman."

Everyone stood in the house, shocked and dismayed, the empty pie plates and half-empty glasses cluttered around the living room and table. Scott's mom was dabbing her eye with a napkin and sobbing. "Oh my, oh my." She was wringing her hands. "I didn't know it was that bad."

Robert stood wavering in the entrance, clearly shaken up, his tie loose around his neck. He was sweating slightly. "Good job, Scott, way to make a problem."

"Ya. Way to play your aces, dumbo," Phillip chimed in. "You knew what you were doing when you made your comments."

"I didn't know anything had happened with the boat until this conversation! I thought the boat was Dad's. And Dad, you know as well as I that it was Owen who ruined that boat, not Matthew."

"I know," Robert admitted. "I still told you very clearly not to cause any problems." He was struggling with what to say, still indecisive. "I'm not saying that was all your fault, but you definitely didn't help."

His dad turned and walked from the room, pacing to the kitchen. He suddenly turned. His face darkened. "Scott, I want you to leave. I'm a man who keeps my word." He turned and walked again. "I'll reconsider whether or not you can stay here in the morning."

His dad opened the screen door and disappeared into the evening darkness. "I want you gone before I get back," he called over his shoulder.

Scott stood speechless in the hall. His dad's truck started and the lights flashed across the front window as he turned down the driveway.

His mom was crying angrily. "Just go, Scott." She turned and thumped up the stairs and slammed the door to her room.

Phillip stood and shrugged his shoulders. "Tough," was all he said, he walked past Scott and disappeared outside. "I'm leaving."

That night as Scott pulled down the driveway, a few fall leaves swirling in his headlights, he felt empty. More then emptiness. He felt something else, too. Maybe it was cockiness, or confidence. He knew where he was going and he was glad to go.

"Dad," Scott said calmly into the darkness. "I wish you well."

The End.

Look for the second part to this exciting series!

Epilogue

Hey, it's Scott again. Thank you for reading about me and sharing my life experience. If you read the book for entertainment, I hope you enjoyed it. There will be more books about my story coming out soon. Just search online for the authors' names or for the name of my book. My life goes in yet another direction later and I can't wait to tell you about it.

I wanted this book written for more than just entertainment. It exists to help you become more trustworthy. While trying not to micromanage, I made sure that the authors progressed carefully, not shoving as many lessons in the book as possible. Therefore, the only lesson in here is to increase your ability to be trusted.

Speaking of the authors, let me introduce the authors to you.

David Allen is 22 years old, and has a business degree. Since he learned about the three legs of trust, he has learned how to gain a network of people he trusts. This network has proven helpful to him in dealing with the deaths of both his parents, who died four months apart from each other. Without constantly working on increasing his trust, he would not have any deep connections with anyone.

Brian Shaul is a life coach who has spent over 10,000 hours working with people one-on-one to improve their lives. He has found that the three legs of trust are the foundation for emotional health. He has found that the people he works with get the results they need, add value to others, learn who to trust, and learn who not to trust when they understand this basic lesson at a heart level.

Now that you have some background information on them, I want you to understand what I mean when I say someone has learned something at a heart level, because this is what makes all the difference.

People can learn a lesson and store it in their head, and can answer correctly if asked a question about it. That is one level of learning, a level with which most of you are familiar. To take action based on that answer is to know that lesson at an even deeper level. Further, to be able to act in accordance with what you've learned without having to think about it is one of the furthest levels at which you can learn anything. I cannot stress the importance of learning at a deep level, especially with issue of character.

I call this deep understanding 'learning at a heart level.'

If you do not learn trust at that heart level, people will be suspicious of you, often without reason. Progress in any endeavor will move very slowly, and problems with people will plague you all the way through your journey. However, if you do learn at an actionable level to live a high-trust life, your little mistakes will cause less suffering, higher trust people will gravitate toward you, and your chances of success are greatly increased.

One great way to learn at a heart level is to study this book and the worksheets that follow in a group. Many who read the book and do the worksheets by themselves will find themselves scoring around 70% or 80%. This is often because we see the world through our eyes only. Studying in a group will increase your perceived capacity to be trustworthy.

In other words, you'll find that you really aren't as trustworthy as you thought, that you actually have a lot of opportunities to improve. Keep in mind that this understanding doesn't make you less trustworthy than before, it just gives you a chance to gain more trust and to better identify trust in others. You may get defensive. If you do, it is because you are letting an emotional wall down, allowing new things to influence how you see the world. Sometimes that is uncomfortable.

I promise you this: Increasing your trust will improve your life, taking you from good to great in all areas where you apply the lessons. I urge you to work on the worksheets as a group and share your own strengths and weaknesses. You are welcome to make copies so that you can repeat them as much as you like, measuring your progress as you go. God Bless You.

— Scott Calloway

Having Integrity

Worksheet #1

Integrity isn't something that you do, its something that you have. Actions that demonstrate any of these six categories to a high degree will increase your integrity in the eyes of others. Faking these characteristics or going completely against them will lower your integrity.

After making copies, circle a number that represents how you see yourself on each of these. For further feedback, have others fill out where they feel you are on each of these anonymously, writing suggestions that you can use for improvement.

1. Patience 1 2 3 4 5 6 7 8 9 10

2. Kindness 1 2 3 4 5 6 7 8 9 10

3. Not envious 1 2 3 4 5 6 7 8 9 10

4. Humility 1 2 3 4 5 6 7 8 9 10

5. Slow to anger 1 2 3 4 5 6 7 8 9 10

6. Truthfulness 1 2 3 4 5 6 7 8 9 10

Total _____/60

Average (total/6)_____

If you have questions or want to email a story about your experience using this worksheet, send an email to "scottthebook@gmail.com"

Getting the Job Done

Worksheet #2

Getting the job done is a little different. Often we test people for trust by seeing if they get the job done for us or not. When people say they will do something, and they do it, your trust for them goes up. If they don't do it, you question whether you should trust them anymore. To truly have trust, you must do more than just care about others and have integrity. You must also be able to take action and get results.

After making copies, circle a number that represents how you see yourself on each of these. For further feedback, have others fill out where they feel you are on each of these anonymously, writing suggestions that you can use for improvement. One suggestion is to figure out for yourself what would meet your needs. What do you value when it comes to achievement? Find out this information from others to increase your score.

1. Do you usually have a plan?

1 2 3 4 5 6 7 8 9 10

2. Do you prioritize well?

1 2 3 4 5 6 7 8 9 10

3. Are you resourceful?

1 2 3 4 5 6 7 8 9 10

4. Can you gain momentum?

1 2 3 4 5 6 7 8 9 10

5. Are you able to follow through?

1 2 3 4 5 6 7 8 9 10

Total _____/50

Average (total/5)_____

If you have questions or want to email a story about your experience using this worksheet, send an email to "scottthebook@gmail.com"

Having Other People's Best Interest In Mind

Worksheet #3

Having another person's best interests in mind means seeing and realizing how your actions will affect that particular person. Once you fill out Worksheet #3, you will have a better understanding of what this means. In order to fill it out, you will need to ask yourself, "Where am I on a scale of 1 to 10 on these behaviors? Out of every ten decisions, how often do I do these things?" Like in golf, your goal is to have a low score for these characteristics. After you find your average, subtract that number from the number 10 to see just how high you rank on a 1-10 scale on having other people's best interest in mind.

Desiring to be Recognized and Appreciated

1 2 3 4 5 6 7 8 9 10

Drawing Attention to my Abilities and Achievements

1 2 3 4 5 6 7 8 9 10

Refusing to Give Up Personal Rights

1 2 3 4 5 6 7 8 9 10

Desiring to Control Others

1 2 3 4 5 6 7 8 9 10

Being Quick to Blame Others for Their Failures

1 2 3 4 5 6 7 8 9 10

Being Self-Focused

1 2 3 4 5 6 7 8 9 10

Becoming Defensive When Criticized

1 2 3 4 5 6 7 8 9 10

Being Overly Concerned About What Others Think of Me

1 2 3 4 5 6 7 8 9 10

Difficulty Admitting When I Have Failed

1 2 3 4 5 6 7 8 9 10

Feeling Hurt When I Am Overlooked

1 2 3 4 5 6 7 8 9 10

Desiring for Others to Meet my Needs

1 2 3 4 5 6 7 8 9 10

Viewing Others as Lower Than Myself

1 2 3 4 5 6 7 8 9 10

Feeling Self-Sufficient With no Need for God or Others

1 2 3 4 5 6 7 8 9 10

Feeling Sorry For Myself Because I'm Not Appreciated

1 2 3 4 5 6 7 8 9 10

Desiring to be Successful Apart From God's Blessing or Direction

1 2 3 4 5 6 7 8 9 10

Total _____/150

Average (total/15)_____

Having Other's Best Interests in Mind
(10- Average) _____

If you have questions or want to email a story about your experience using this worksheet, send an email to "scottthebook@gmail.com"

Your Total Score

Worksheet #4

This worksheet puts everything together. Practice this on yourself first, because you are about to do this exercise several times on the last sheet. For further feedback, have others fill out anonymously where they feel you are on each of these, writing suggestions that you can use for improvement. Of course, people who trust each other very highly may be more open if they are comfortable.

Average of Integrity

=___

Average of Getting the Job Done

=___

(10- Average)Other People's Best Interests In Mind

=___

Total = ___/30

Average (total/3) =___

If you have questions or want to email a story about your experience using this worksheet, send an email to "scottthebook@gmail.com"

Who Do You Trust?

Worksheet #5

In Worksheet #5 you can diagram your friends and see if they have the three legs of trust. Just ask all the below questions about your friends.

Does this person have integrity?
Does this person get the job done?
Does this person have other people's best interests in mind? Do they have yours?
What are their strengths, and what are their weaknesses in each area?

Sometimes, making a guess based upon your gut feeling can be a valuable starting point for gaining awareness. After that, use the previous sheets for guidance on what areas could use improvement. Then you will have valuable feedback you could give to these people if they asked for it.

If your friends are in your study group, it will require strong emotional intelligence to do this openly. I recommend doing it anonymously for yourself, first, if the trust environment is low or people are uncomfortable with that level of transparency. More benefit will come doing this openly with your most trusted friends if the level of trust and comfort are already high.

Name: _____   Name: _____
Integrity: _____   Integrity: _____
Job Done: _____   Job Done: _____
Best Interest: _____ Best Interest: _____
Average: _____   Average: _____

Name: _____   Name: _____
Integrity: _____   Integrity: _____
Job Done: _____   Job Done: _____
Best Interest: _____ Best Interest: _____
Average: _____   Average: _____

If you have questions or want to email a story about your experience using this worksheet, send an email to "scottthebook@gmail.com"

Keep reading for a sneak peek at events in the next book in the **Emotionally Bulletproof** *series…*

At the sound of loud knocking, Jean Calloway opened the door.

"Ma'am, I'm Detective Tom Hoffman. Is Robert Calloway at this address?" the man at the door asked.

Robert was still in his suit and tie from work. He got up from the living room couch, and made his way to the door. "I'll handle this, Jean."

Jean stood, unsure of herself for a moment, then went into the kitchen to stir the boiling pot of spaghetti noodles cooking on the stove.

"So, what's a detective doing at my doorstep? Is there really so little happening in this town that you have to do DUI-related house visits normally given to the regular men in blue?"

Detective Hoffman's brows lowered slightly, unsure of whether Mr. Calloway was merely being conversational, or insulting. "Mr. Calloway, I am not here for drunk driving. I am here on a murder investigation." He handed Robert several pieces of paper stapled together. "I have some questions for you, so I'll explain it as briefly as possible so I can get down to business."

Robert looked up from the papers he now held.

"On 9:30 a.m. yesterday, Tiffany Davis filed a restraining order against her husband, Owen Davis, on the grounds that she had been threatened and feared for her life. We have documented evidence from two nights ago by Officer Fisk and Officer Houghes that while detaining Mr. Davis on the highway, Mrs. Davis and Scott Calloway, your son, pulled up in front of Mr. Davis's stopped car. As Mrs. Tiffany Davis attempted to talk to her husband, he threatened to kill her. He was reported to have said, while very intoxicated: 'I'll shut you up for good, you nagging woman. I've done it before with your last husband; you know I can do it again.'"

"Owen was drunk. That quantity of alcohol can affect the prefrontal cortex of the brain, responsible for logic and sound judgment. In those conditions, anybody can say things that are hurtful, or don't make sense at all." Robert was immediately on the defensive for his best friend.

"I'm not finished, Mr. Calloway. This is a murder investigation. I am here because Mr. Davis is a murder suspect. His wife, Tiffany, came into the Wasilla police station yesterday morning to file a restraining order, accompanied by your son. They gave us information that Matthew Tanner, her previous husband, died in a construction accident. Your son, an assistant manager of his company at that time, confirmed Mr. Davis as the foreman of that company. Seeing as Mr. Davis has full ownership of the company and is married to Matthew's former wife, there is possible motivation."

Robert quickly mustered the skillful, convincing voice he developed in psychology. "Thomas, Owen knew more about the running of the business than anybody else. I would even argue that during the marital trouble Matthew had at that time, and his irrational distraction with trying to teach unproven religious psychology, Owen came to know even more than Matthew. Tiffany gave Owen the company because she knew about his knowledge and expertise. I agreed with her that due to this, Owen was the best man for keeping Matthew's pride and joy alive."

Detective Hoffman pointed to the papers in Robert's hand. "The first three pages are a police report, but you need to look at this."

Robert flipped the first three papers over, revealing what looked like printouts of journal entries. Certain places in the handwritten pages were highlighted, allowing Robert to skim over it quickly.

"— July 4, 1988: Today we had a family picnic... Unknown to me, my brother-in-law invited Owen, my foreman. I of course had to play along, not showing that I hadn't wanted him to come. My brother-in-law was talking with him like he owned the company. It makes me wonder just how close Owen and Robert are to each other?! I felt very put out, like they are in a small gang together and they both don't like me...I need to confront my foreman about the money that keeps disappearing, but I think I'll wait until I've given him enough rope to hang himself"

" —July 27, 1988: I think my foreman is having an affair with my wife—"

"August 10, 1988: I'm going to challenge Owen tomorrow. I think I finally have enough evidence that he can't deny it... My company is working...four-story apartment building, I will have to inspect the site with Owen after the work is done and I believe that will be a good time...I'll ask him where the material is, then I will confront him about the other materials and fire him if he cannot show me ...where all of it is."

"I've never seen this before in my life!" Robert was stunned. *How could something like this still be around five years after Matthew's death?* he thought.

"This is a copy of a journal with Matthew's handwriting on it. We matched the handwriting with documents he filled out before his death, which was on the day the journal claims Matthew had confronted Owen. The journal places both Matthew and Owen alone at the job site. Tiffany claimed she had married Owen three weeks after Matthew's death, not sure of what to do with the company, and you, the best man at the wedding, recommended his promotion from foreman to owner/operator. Is that correct?"

Robert straightened his tie. "Look, Owen was friends with me since high school, I had no idea that foul play was involved. Sure, I didn't like Matthew very much, but the last thing I want to do is jeopardize my practice and my standing in the community by associating myself with that kind of behavior. I trusted Owen, but it seems here you never...you know... you never really know a person that well." Beads of sweat dripped down Robert's face. He never intended to kill anyone, it was the furthest thought from his mind. The detective didn't know that, however, and now the conversation was not going in the direction he had hoped.

"Connect the dots, Mr. Calloway. It looks very incriminating for Owen, and the facts don't absolve you from suspicion of being connected. If I were you, I would take this situation much more seriously. Do you know what the penalty is for accessory to murder?"

Robert's throat felt dry. He had things to say. He could say that he cared about his sister and he wouldn't knowingly support a wedding between a murderer and his own sister. He could repeat his conviction of Owen being the most experienced worker, and that his promotion was a rational decision. Above all that raced through his mind, he knew that his words, no matter how honest, put him in a defensive position, therefore making his situation worse. The last thing he wanted was to get handcuffed by the officer waiting in the car and hauled to the police station in front of his own wife at his own home. He wished he could have talked to Scott about this beforehand. Maybe he had been too hard on his son.

Either way, Robert decided upon the most cooperative option he could choose without incriminating himself.

"Owen's recent behavior with my sister has worried me. It caused my family a lot of tension in the last few days. This new information, even if most of it isn't concrete, does make the situation worse. I seriously question whether I want him around my sister, and I definitely don't want him around me, if he's that much trouble. What can I do to prove to you without a doubt that my family and I have no connection to Owen, or his actions?"

The detective leaned forward slightly. His crime-seeking expression remained intact, but he seemed somewhat relaxed. Robert immediately felt some of his own nervousness depart. There was a chance to get out of this bad situation after all. Finally, the detective spoke.

"There is a high chance that Owen will be convicted. He will go to jail, either for criminal threatening or murder. You don't want to be associated with either crime, do you?"

Robert knew when to shut up. Even he recognized an authority figure when he saw one, and so the detective continued uninterrupted.

"Be at the station at 9:00 a.m. tomorrow morning. You will answer questions, telling us everything you know. If you cooperate, we will have the strong case against Owen that we need. Once we have what we need, we obviously won't need you to stay any longer. I will warn you, however, that refusal to answer questions or to show up at all will be incriminating against you, should we choose to pursue that course. To make sure I'm clear, you do not want to give me any reason to implicate you, and failure to comply will definitely give reason. Complying, on the other hand, will reduce our need to attach jail time, community service, or public record of criminal activity to your name. Do you understand?"

"Y-Yes officer," Robert stuttered for possibly the first time in several years. "I'll be there."

Three minutes later, Robert collapsed on the couch. He felt the need for a distraction, but he avoided turning on the television. He felt that easing his mind, even a little, would only contribute to the danger he faced. Jean noticed the awkward silence as she returned from the kitchen with a plate of freshly made spaghetti and several slices of buttered bread.

She gave him his food without a word, and after collecting her own plate of food, joined him in the living room.

Robert looked down at the meal in front of him, saying nothing. The conversation continued in his mind. *All right Robert, skip the depression, anger, pleading, all that bull. Just figure out what needs to be done. I have two choices here. Put my best friend behind bars, possibly for life, or possibly go down with him. Even if I don't go to jail, if people talk about this at all, and they will if this goes to court, then my clients will go to the other psychologists. It looks like I have to go. If I don't, the money situation will definitely be worse than it is right now...How did I get into this mess? After I helped him get a job and everything, this is how he repays me..."*

Robert looked up and saw his wife sitting next to him. "Honey, did you hear the detective?"

Jean finished chewing and answered. "I wanted to, but at the same time I was afraid to hear, so I just went back to the kitchen. All I got was that there was a murder investigation."

"Owen may have been part of something ugly. The detectives want me to come in and answer questions. They think Matthew's death wasn't an accident."

Jean, who had felt apprehensive about the wedding happening between Owen and Tiff, had similar thoughts, but thought it best not to voice them until now.

"The more I see him, the more aggressive and scary he seems to be. I can't help but sympathize for your sister." She noticed that the sense of control Robert usually had over situations seemed absent, and she felt empathy for her husband that was just as rare as his lack of control. "Will you be all right?" she asked.

"Fine. Fine. I know what I need to do."